1

CW01501109

     In the rich dark of the ＿ dotted with a millions tiny suns, the endless Redwood Forest came alive with the sounds of life from every branch and treetop, every shrub and hollow, and every nook and cranny. The woodlands teemed and buzzed and chirped as a chill breeze swept through their branches and leaves, shaking and ruffling the canopies into a vast rumbling ocean of deep, lustrous red breaks and swells.

     The ground rustled underfoot with thousands of fallen leaves as a small herd of deer picked their way cautiously through the trees, their slumber that night having been disturbed by two shadows stalking through the thick trunks.

     The shadows stood upon two feet, and moved most definitely as though they didn't belong amidst the trees. And indeed, nothing had changed. None other than those of Featherstone origin were welcomed amongst the Redwoods, and so these two strangers moved as warily as possible in the darkness, all too aware that they should not have been there.

     It was however, their profession, and they made similar guarded journeys such as this almost every night. They were poachers, and they were among the very few remaining still in the occupation, and they had certainly not retained their position by being reckless.

     Between them they carried as much equipment as they could manage, but at the same time, only the bare essentials. It was a fine line to walk to make their illegal journeys worthwhile and profitable, but as the same time be light enough to make a hasty escape, should the need ever arise.

They each shifted the weight of two large, spring loaded bear traps, with huge, gaping, metal jaws and razor sharp teeth. Food and water of course they needed too, for they were often out all night and into the early hours of the morning. And, finally, several rolls of snare wire they each also had stuffed into their pockets.

Years of poaching had taught them to move almost silently through the woodlands without sacrificing speed. Of course, compared to the animals who made their homes here, they would never be a match, but as far as humans went, they were among the best.

Stopping suddenly between two thick tree trunks and crouching down low, one of the men made several signals and signs with his hands to the other, barely even distinguishable in the dark of the night. The second man nodded and crouched down also, kneeling beside his partner, silently sliding one of the heavy bear traps from his shoulder as he did so.

It took them barely three minutes to lay the trap, set it, and cover it with a thin layer of soil and dirt to disguise its presence. Their practiced hands moved precisely and without hesitation, regardless of the fact that they were passing repeatedly through such a dangerous mechanism: not dangerous to them though, only to whatever poor creature came along and stepped on it.

The Redwoods Rise and Fall

Ever since Vivian Featherstone had returned, many things had changed. Poaching in any form had swiftly been made illegal, with Vivian seeking out many of the poachers herself. But in Astley and Zander's eyes, these two particularly proficient poachers, that simply meant that their prizes fetched higher prices, once they had found the right buyer of course.

Vivian's sudden and overwhelming presence in Virtus had scared many of their customers into hiding, and it was only the gutsiest and greediest amongst them who still bought from the two criminals.

Yes, Vivian had changed many things indeed.

"Done." Astley whispered to his partner, though in the darkness the sound still carried away between the trees.

"Keep your voice down you idiot!" Zander breathed in reply, though his voice was still clearly harsh and worn.

"There's no one here." Astley mumbled submissively, though indeed his response was barely even a breath. "Are we going to lay all four?" He asked, shifting the weight of the remaining bear trap slung over his shoulder and eyeing the two his partner was still carrying.

"Of course we are!" Zander snapped back at him, his eyes flitting over with annoyance to Astley in the darkness. "Now shut up and come on!"

Astley didn't reply, simply following Zander off into the dark of the woods once more, leaving their set trap behind them, and only making a mental note of its location so they could check it again later.

Just as he stepped off to leave however, seeing Zander's silhouette barely visible ahead of him, he stopped and turned for a moment, casting a glance all around. There was a rustling in the bushes off to his left, and a cool breeze whipped past him to the right. The hairs on the back of his neck and on his arms stood on end, and the horrible feeling of being watched formed a pit in his stomach.

Finally he pushed the feeling aside and hurried silently after his overbearing partner, knowing that if he delayed any longer he would surely once again suffer the wrath of Zander's sharp tongue.

The two of them were out of sight within seconds, and then out of earshot within minutes, and so neither of them saw or heard what happened next.

The great metal jaws, hidden beneath the light dusting of earth and the fallen leaves, began to creak and shudder and groan. The small square pressure plate, protruding up only slightly higher than the rest of the contraption, was only just visible, whilst the rest of the device, including the hulking teeth and spring mechanism, were all concealed beneath.

Suddenly the trap triggered, and the monstrous manmade teeth ripped from below the soil with blinding speed, clamping together with awful force and a terrifying crack. Animals and birds screamed and screeched into flight, fleeing instinctively in every direction away from the murdering monstrosity.

The Redwoods Rise and Fall

Nothing had stepped on the plate however, and the great jaws had caught only air. They hovered there for a few more moments, sealed tightly shut, rattling and vibrating from the force of their own strength. But then, the strange pressure that had forced the trap to trigger in the first place intensified once more. It bore down upon the strong arms like a heavy burden, unrelenting, and the creaking and groaning grew ever louder.

Eventually it all became too much, and with a horrible grinding and crunching sound, the awful trap buckled and collapsed in on itself, mashed and crushed into a wrecked ball, now nothing but a useless hunk of metal.

With a glimmer of satisfaction in her eyes, yet another shadowy human figure darted away through the trees, only this one was welcome amongst the woodlands, instead of being feared by them.

The figure slipped between the trees as if it belonged there, unseen and unheard.

"Did you hear that?" Astley whispered to his partner, breaking the automatic silence they had adopted since leaving their last laid trap. He stopped and cocked his ear to the wind, certain he had heard a crack on the breeze.

"Hear what?" Zander snapped back, irritated that his fool of a partner was speaking once again.

"That noise. Like a crack." Astley mumbled, still straining his ears.

"There was no noise you fool. You probably stood on a branch, you moron." Zander replied with an exasperated sigh, apparently mortally wounded by his partner's total incompetence.

Astley ignored his brute of a partner's last comment.

"I don't like it tonight." He commented then, more to himself than to Zander. "It doesn't feel right. Something's definitely wrong."

Zander didn't reply to that final comment, not even with a sigh. He muttered something inaudible under his breath about Astley being a superstitious moron, before continuing on, quickening his pace.

He grunted in frustration as he broke three twigs with his next five steps, distracted by his own cynicism.

Their carelessness however, though it might have been brief, cost them their stealth dearly, and a barely visible shape shifted scarcely an inch or so amongst the shadow of the trees, unseen as ever in the night of the Redwoods.

As Astley and Zander turned their backs, hurrying on with the rest of their night's work, the silhouette turned silently to follow, moving just enough to reveal a set of shining blue eyes, trained maliciously on the two poachers.

Their energetic light had been dimmed drastically by time, and by sombre obligation, and the harsh stare that they now cast was full of anger and hate and lust and vengeance.

2

"Miss Featherstone. I'm sorry but this issue really must be addressed..." Archer repeated in something of exasperation, his voice worn down by time and by his profession, and his patience too worn thin by Vivian's tremendous task.

He had for as long as he could remember been an advisor to the Featherstone family. When he'd lived under Miranda and Dorian's roof at Featherstone Keep, he'd always travelled with them to counsel, and he had known Vivian since the day she was born.

The assassination attempt had very nearly claimed his life, but having lived in the Keep for so long, he had memorised all of the best escape routes. He was no fool, and he had always known the Greystones would be trouble, though he could never have imagined quite how much trouble.

The years he had spent under their rule in the city, now known to all as Virtus, had not been good years, for he had practically had to go into hiding. Those of Featherstone allegiance had all been put to execution, including those loyal to them in the House. It was not a very productive way to spend one's time, but it had certainly served the Greystone's purpose, and their reign had been absolute.

That was, at least, until young Vivian had showed up and usurped them. Of course, the second Archer had learned of this, he had sought out young

Vivian and immediately come to her aid. He wanted to help restore Virtus to its original splendour.

He had felt for some reason almost obliged to do so, having served the Featherstones for so long. There had been absolutely no way he could sit back and do nothing.

He was still tall and slender and, he liked to think, even more intelligent, for admittedly, his mind was sharp as ever, though his slicked back black hair was now more than a little tinged with grey.

"Archer…" Vivian began, her patience too a little taxed. "I've already asked you, I don't know how many times, please don't call me that. It was always Vivian. I would like it to always be Vivian."

Young Vivian Featherstone, the last remaining survivor of their legendary bloodline, daughter to the murdered Dorian and Miranda Featherstone, and to the great red mother bear, Clover, and friend to her dearest murdered Red, was a very different young woman to the one who had returned to Virtus, over five years ago.

Now in her early twenties, Vivian's mind and body had developed both, and she had blossomed into a gorgeous and intelligent young woman. Her hair was still the same shade of brown, streaked with lighter, glimmering shades, but whilst time had on one hand developed her, it had also worn her down. Her once bright blue eyes had been dimmed and pained by the slow, painful passage of time, and by the enormity and scale of her task, and everything that came with it.

Considering the difficulty and complexity of her task, she had been eternally grateful when Archer had appeared and offered her his experience in the field of management.

"I'm sorry Vivian…" He hastily apologised. "Forgive me, but we really must address these matters."

"I know, Archer, I know. I'm sorry…" Vivian apologised in turn, and tried her best to focus her weary mind.

"The economy is still rising." He continued, deciding to switch subjects quickly to try to capture her attention.

His tactic had worked - he did indeed capture Vivian's attention, but unfortunately, for all the wrong reasons.

"Yes, Archer, I know." Vivian replied immediately, her voice edgy and her eyes flinty. "And a lot of that's due to poaching. There are still some I haven't had the time to find. The ones who don't seem to care that it's now illegal."

"If I may Vivian…" Archer continued, his voice wavering and faltering slightly, though he chased his point nonetheless. "Perhaps you should leave them be?"

"What?" She asked slowly, her eyes darkening and her tone growing dangerous.

"They're helping Virtus continue to grow and flourish." He quickly attempted to justify. "Surely a few can't hurt?"

But as soon as those final words had left his lips, Archer realised he had erred, and the withering look that Vivian gave him then chilled him to the very core, for her will was something to be both feared and respected, and he daren't cross her. Though, of course, she had never wronged him: it just wasn't in her nature to do so. But still, why would any man go out of his way to upset the most powerful woman in the world?

It simply wasn't worth it.

"No." Was all she said at first, uttering the word slowly and carefully and coldly, ensuring that Archer was in absolutely no doubt that he was testing her patience quite severely.

"I…I thought that…I, maybe it might help with the problem the farmers on the outskirts are having? To the south, something's killing their cattle…I thought they might be able to catch the beast, whatever it is." He attempted.

"No. Poaching." Vivian repeated then, emphasising her words very slowly and very clearly, her voice heavy with the weight of absolute finality, and Archer knew much better than to argue.

"Vivian…I…apologise…"

"Don't apologise Archer." She replied sternly, cutting him off. "But never suggest anything like that, ever again. Understand?"

"Yes." He agreed immediately. "Of course."

"Good." She accepted, though her words were still sharp. "Anything else?"

"I…I don't think…" He stammered, losing track of the long list he'd had stored in his mind.

"Good. That will be all then. Goodnight Archer."

Apparently having run aground, the quick witted man knew an easy exit when he saw one, and knew after the err he had made he would make no further progress today.

He inclined his head respectfully and started for the front door to Vivian's house.

"Goodnight Vivian." That was all he said as he left, closing the chipped and scratched white wooden door behind him and descending the few steps that made up Vivian's porch.

She watched him head immediately right and hurry down the street back to his own home, barely a mile or so off to the west. Vivian sighed heavily and collapsed wearily into a wooden armchair, padded with but a few meagre cushions.

For the most powerful woman in the world, young Vivian did not live as many might have expected. She lived pretty much directly in the centre of Virtus, which in of itself was not unusual in the slightest, since she was unofficially tasked with the running of the city. But she did not live in a castle, nor a mansion, or anything of the sort in fact.

She lived in a small, one bedroom house, painted entirely white and squeezed, just as all the other houses on that road were, between two other equally squashed houses on either side.

The wooden planks and timbers that kept it together were rotten in places, and creaked and groaned with even the faintest breeze. But none of that mattered. She didn't need a great, hulking mansion of a house. She was barely ever there anyway.

Her main concern was not the quality of her own life, but instead the quality of the lives' of the people of Virtus, and of the inhabitants of the Redwood Forest. They had become her only focus. Vivian had lost everything that meant anything to her already anyway, so she had dedicated herself wholly to this task, and would not rest until she knew it no longer required her attention.

Darkness crept slowly over the mixture of wooden and slate and stone rooftops, some with chimneys that spewed smoke into the dimming night sky, and others that simply provided protection from the elements.

The virtus of the people: 'The People's Power'. That was all Vivian had known of this place for so long. All those years she had spent hiding from mankind, from the Greystones. She had never once during that time imagined that one day the people of this city would refer to her as 'The People's Power'.

It was apt, she supposed, and reasonably accurate.

But she wasn't the true virtus of the people, as, in time, she would come to realise.

That was something else entirely.

At first she had made all of the decisions herself, not wanting to trust anyone with anything important, wishing to ensure that everything she did was fair and just and perfect. It didn't take long however for her to realise that this approach simply wasn't feasible for her to maintain, and so with time she adapted and altered her approach to 'ruling'.

Never had she considered herself a queen or a ruler, or anything of the sort. The thought of it made her sick to the stomach. She wanted her people to be free to live their own lives. They were only her people just as much as they were indeed each other's. They simply looked to her for guidance.

The Redwoods Rise and Fall

Some of the Lords and Ladies of the old House had survived the Greystone rule, but, admittedly, not many, and only those who had been faithfully loyal to the Grey.

Those that had been still loyal to the Featherstones, and in turn had tried to organise a search party for young Vivian, had swiftly been executed under the Grey's order.

Therefore, Vivian had decided that half of the problem was that when people with power were given more power, and more authority, it often went to their heads. And so, she had made the decision to form an altogether new House. But, as of yet, she had absolutely no idea where to start.

Darkness closed in completely over the next half an hour or so then, and the hustle and bustle in the street outside died down. Vivian clambered up the wooden stairs cutting along the side of her house, leading to the single bedroom and bathroom upstairs, the steps creaking terribly as she climbed.

Her bedroom was simple and plain, just as her room had been in Featherstone Keep, all those years ago. There was a single canvas decorating the one wall opposite her bed, and as Vivian clambered into her groaning, wooden poster bed, she looked over the canvas briefly as she did every night.

It depicted the skyline over a mountain range, streaking sunset rays of orange and yellow and red across the purple and blue and grey faces of the mountains. There were also a few birds pictured crossing the striking lines of colour, soaring high in the skies, though what they were exactly it was difficult to make out.

She didn't really know why she looked it over each night. Perhaps it was because that simple act reminded her of a life she had long lost.

Sighing deeply, the beautiful, burdened young woman closed her eyes and settled into her cold bed, pondering the issue of what she would do about her problem of deciding on a new House, and not for the first time, she drifted away into a deep, troubled sleep.

3

Vivian sat amongst the trees contentedly, whistling quietly to herself a tune from her childhood that she had at one point long forgotten. Preparing her fire to begin cooking, her stomach rumbled deeply and she placed her hand there gently for a moment to quieten it.

'Not long now' she thought silently to herself, for she knew that Red was on his way back with a catch.

"Hungry?" Clover's powerful, caring voice echoed softly from beside her, the great red mother bear ambling gracefully into view of the clearing within which Vivian sat.

"We've been hungrier." Vivian replied honestly, shrugging her shoulders almost casually. Clover sat down beside her young daughter and smiled whimsically.

"Very true." She agreed. "We've been on tough times…"

Vivian sighed deeply then and pulled her flint out from her pocket. Striking the stone a few times, she soon caught a spark on the kindling she had prepared. A swift breeze whipped through the clearing then and sent her flames roaring to life.

"What happened to us Clover?" She asked her mother then, regret ingrained deeply in her voice. "Things could have been so different. What did I do wrong?"

"It was nothing you did my dear." Clover assured her comfortingly. "It was simply the way things were meant to be."

Vivian sighed again.

"Really? If it's supposed to be this way, then why have I lost everything?"

"You haven't." Clover said then in a very matter of fact way. "You still have a very important purpose."

"It's not fair." Vivian concluded rather lamely, knowing even as she uttered the words that fairness didn't come into this equation. She always considered such things when concerned with her people, or with the Redwoods, but seldom were such generosities reciprocated.

"It very rarely is." Clover admitted sadly, echoing Vivian's thoughts almost exactly. "But what else must we do, if not what we're supposed to?"

"Hmm…" Vivian half agreed, though she was by no means convinced.

"What would you have changed, Vivian?" Her mother bear asked then, cocking her head slightly to one side and raising one eyebrow inquisitively, if a bear is even able to do so.

"We would still be living together, in the Redwoods." Vivian replied immediately, without even a moment's hesitation. "I would never have lost you or Red…"

"But what in the world could you have done differently Vivian?" Clover asked her then. "It was all the Greystone's doing, not yours. You had no choice."

"I don't know…" Vivian admitted, dropping her head slightly, knowing deep down of course that Clover was right.

The light padding of careful footsteps drew their attention then and they turned their heads to see Red materialising from between the trees, his thick coat such a perfect match for the colour of the trunks all around that it seemed as though he literally walked through them. He held a deer between his jaws, an adult, but still of course no problem for him to carry alone, for now he was fully grown, well fed, and had no equal that Vivian could imagine.

"Red." She greeted him automatically, rising to her feet and going straight to him, her muscles acting on their own, completely without thought.

He deposited his prize carefully beside the fire and looked to his Vivian.

"Viv." He replied affectionately.

She wrapped her arms immediately around his thick neck, running her fingers through his heavy, soft fur, feeling the warmth radiating from him. She closed her eyes and sighed, burying her face too in his welcoming coat. She had missed this feeling, having been denied it for so long.

"You know you really can't blame yourself for what happened Viv…" He said gently, resting his massive snout lightly on her shoulder as she embraced him. "You've got to stop it. You'll make yourself ill."

"I know." She sighed. "You've said…"

She stayed there for a moment, unwilling to move, blissfully content. Her arms tightened around

Red's neck and held him ever more firmly, wishing fervently that she could hold him forever.

But, as Clover had so aptly pointed out, it was never meant to be.

Sadly, Vivian had already had that time of her life. As much as she might have adored it, now it was passed, and there was nothing she could do about it.

Suddenly, her arms flailed forward and Vivian's hands caught each other. She jerked to stop herself from falling and, opening her eyes, Vivian saw that she was left holding nothing. Red had vanished. She looked to her side and behind her, and saw that Clover was gone too.

The fire at her feet snuffed out then, leaving only a thin wisp of smoke and a chilling breeze that formed a great chasm in the pit of Vivian's stomach.

It was all that she had ever feared.

A sudden break in the clouds above cast a few fleeting rays of moonlight down upon the clearing they had chosen to rest in, illuminating the terrible truth that she had been trying to mask.

Either side of her now, lit up amidst the darkness, were the figures of two bears, both black. Infected by the plague, Red and Clover's carcasses lay at Vivian's feet, motionless, lifeless.

She looked upon their corpses for a moment, her breath caught in her throat, unable to move, or even breathe. Vivian's muscles were frozen in place, all comprehension of anything besides sheer horror and devastation gone.

Then something released inside of her, something vaguely resembling acceptance, and she opened her mouth with a piercing scream, echoing the high-pitched shriek through the trees and out over the entire Redwood Empire endlessly.

Screaming and bolting to sit upright in her bed, Vivian choked and gagged for breath. Sweat poured from her and her sheets were saturated in the stuff. Her mouth was dry and her throat croaked, parched and overused.

Breathing quickly and heavily for a few minutes, desperately trying to catch her breath and come to her senses, Vivian pulled her legs from beneath the covers and swivelled to sit on the side of the bed, resting her feet upon the cold wooden floor.

It certainly wasn't the first time she'd awoken from a nightmare. In fact, it was a regular occurrence. Nonetheless, it never got any easier, and it always took her some time to regain herself and steady her racing heart.

Making her way to the bathroom on unsteady feet, Vivian navigated her way through the darkness, rubbing her eyes wearily as she did so. Her night terrors left her sleep deprived and drained, and over time this took a heavy toll on her body, leaving her feeling forever exhausted.

But there was nothing she could do about it.

They were simply something she had to live with.

After splashing her face with cold water and steadying her racing heart, she made her way purposefully back into her bedroom and set about changing her bed sheets in a robotic fashion. That took her all of about two minutes, and then she immediately made for the window.

Looking through the hollow square of dirtied glass briefly before she opened it, she saw that the street below was dark and empty, and far on the horizon the first simmers of dawn were creeping their way over the city, though barely visible still, lighting the blackness all around only ever so slightly.

She clambered out through the window, squeezing carefully through the narrow gap, and grasped the tiles of the edge of her house's rooftop. Hauling herself up over the ledge, hanging there precariously for a moment before she managed to shift her weight forwards, Vivian shimmied up onto the tiled roof.

From there, once she had surpassed the most dangerous part of her ascent, she climbed to the very top of the slanted surface and turned to sit facing the east. And there she waited, watching as the first rays of that morning's sunrise snuck over the horizon, bathing the view of Virtus before her in beautiful morning light. Beyond the city the streaks of orange and yellow danced gracefully over the Redwood Forest's treetops, transforming the sea of trees into a flowing and majestic ocean of colour.

She sat there for about an hour, as she did most mornings, taking in the view wholly and completely, sometimes with tears streaking openly down her face, and pondering everything that the sight brought with it.

Rooftops and chimneys were alighted as if they were aflame, and reflections from a thousand and more glass windows sparkled red and yellow and glorious orange upon Vivian's unprotected face. It was a sight that always brought her great satisfaction, and equally great sorrow.

Later that day, once the sun had risen fully and was high in the sky, after Vivian had watched the awakening of Virtus and the beginnings of the day's bustling activity, for the thousandth time, she left the confines of her house and headed out into the city.

The city itself was much changed from when she had first returned here to kill the Greystones. For starters, and most obviously, it was no longer the ruined mess it had been before. Where once rubble had been strewn about from the Greystone's apparent temper tantrums, roads had been cleared and repaved, houses had been rebuilt and restored, and shops and businesses had sprung up.

Whilst, of course, Vivian had had a hand in the building of many of the first-restored structures, she had certainly not been responsible for them all. She had very quickly realised that, whilst her initial displays of power and kindness were well received, she needed to get the people to work, and allow them to earn their own freedom.

Therefore, the vast majority of the reparations had been completed by the people themselves, making them indeed much more self-sufficient.

"Vivian! Vivian!" A voice sounded then from a little ways down the street, flurrying with alarm.

Of course, being only reasonably self-sufficient meant that whenever a new problem arose, something that the people had not faced before, their first port of call was naturally Vivian.

"Clara!?" Vivian piped, shocked by her old friend's sudden and fleeting arrival. The pretty young girl of about Vivian's age, only very slightly older, was red faced and out of breath from running. She spluttered slightly as she approached, trying desperately to get her words out and breathe at the same time.

As you would expect, considering Clara's panicked state, Vivian feared the worst. Ever since she'd met Clara, all those years ago now when she'd awoken after bawling herself to sleep in Red's dead fur, she had kept in contact with her quite regularly.

Vivian shuddered at the memory of Red's death and quickly moved on.

"What's wrong Clara!? What's going on!?"

"It's Milo! The pipes!"

"What?" Vivian questioned, bewildered. "Milo? Pipes?"

"He's been trying to fit those water pipes again!" Clara attempted to hurriedly explain.

Vivian remembered then the last time she'd seen Clara that her father Milo had been experimenting with pumping water through various pipes into houses. It hadn't ended particularly well, resulting in him almost flooding their house. And by the sounds of it, his latest endeavour had ended pretty much the same way.

"He managed to fit them, but now they've burst! Our house is flooded!"

Vivian released a slow breath, sighing with relief. She had expected much worse news and relaxed inwardly, though she didn't let this show to

Clara, for she could clearly see that her dear friend was devastated.

"How bad is it?" Vivian asked.

"He hasn't been able to shut the pipes off this time! He can't get to them behind the walls!" Clara explained quickly, her voice rising several octaves with each fresh breath. "The whole of downstairs is flooded!"

"Oh…" Vivian responded involuntarily. "I see."

It seemed that actually things were much worse than the last time.

"Show me." She instructed, and almost without even a nod of comprehension, Clara turned on her heels and took off the way she had come from, with Vivian in immediate pursuit.

They reached Clara's house in a matter of minutes, for luckily it wasn't far away. Even at first glance Vivian saw the extent of the damage, and a very bewildered looking Milo stood amidst it all, clothes sodden and clinging to him as he moved.

His head was bald with only a few grey wisps of hair here and there, and his frame was lean, though clearly he had been well built as a younger man, for his body was tough and worn.

"I don't understand…" He was muttering to himself. "I just don't…" He cut off, looking up mid-mutterings and spotting his daughter with the fabled Vivian Featherstone. His expression was one of both surprise and shame, having Vivian witness his second and somewhat much more dramatic failure.

"Milo." She greeted him simply, nodding her head as she approached, Clara in tow now.

"I...I didn't mean for..." He started, obviously embarrassed.

Of course it was not Vivian's intention to embarrass the poor soul, for he was an experienced and proud gentleman, and a very good father, but tinkering almost always requires trial and error to perfect. It was just unfortunate that this error had resulted in the flooding of his own home.

"I'm sure you didn't Milo." Vivian reassured him with a smile, placing her hand on his shoulder and glancing briefly back over her shoulder to Clara. "But you must take more care. Look how upset your daughter is. You've flooded her home, and your own."

"But it was all working..."

"And I don't doubt that for a second." Vivian agreed. "It's a marvellous idea, it would make things much easier. But perhaps you should trial elsewhere? An empty barn perhaps?" She added, quite firmly, and he quickly nodded in agreement, his eyes flitting to his distraught daughter, her gaze upon their ruined home.

"I'm sorry." He quickly apologised.

"Very well." Vivian concluded, much more light heartedly, having solved the issue of practicing reasonably easily. "Now then..."

She then turned her attention to the flooded home of her dear friends, father and daughter. It was built of a mixture of stone and timber, much like many of the houses in the city. This one was on two floors, and water drained here and there and dribbled this way and that between the tiniest cracks and splits in the walls of the ground floor.

The Redwoods Rise and Fall

It would have been pointless to go inside; Vivian could see much better from out here. She closed her eyes and scanned over the structure of the building with her mind, seeing the whole thing in its entirety, strengths and weaknesses, cracks and leaks, in a matter of seconds.

Milo, it seemed, had fed water pipes through the very walls themselves and beneath the floor, having dug the ground up in long, thin trenches, in order to achieve his goal of giving the house running water.

In fact, Vivian was very impressed, for he had come remarkably close to success. Most of what he'd done had actually held firm. She could feel the pressure of the water building and rising and then dropping and falling in different places throughout his system. He was definitely on the right lines, and if he could perfect his method, Vivian knew that the people of Virtus would begin to flurry with new ideas in his wake.

It seemed advancement and revolution was on the horizon: a revolution for which she would not be required.

His only problem, however, was quite simply a weakness in his piping, which had subsequently burst, allowing his system to drain, sadly, directly into their house.

Working quickly, Vivian did not fix the pipe, but instead she drained the water off away from the house, silently 'encouraging' it to flood off down the streets and disappear, soaking into the ground, spreading far and wide.

Then, seeing quite clearly the damage the water had left behind, she removed any sign that there had ever been a flood, sealing all of the cracks in the walls that had been widened, and instantly drying perfectly everything that had been stained. This, of course, would have been impossible without her powers, but such was her advantage.

Eventually she relaxed and opened her eyes, turning to Clara and Milo as she did so.

"There." Was all she said at first, looking to Clara, indicating with that simple comment that she had fixed all that had been wrong.

"Oh thank you Vivian!" Clara exclaimed, throwing her arms around Vivian's neck and embracing her gratefully.

"Milo." Vivian uttered then, turning to Clara's father. He dropped his head and flushed in embarrassment.

"I know…" He began, but Vivian cut him off.

"No, no." She reassured him. "You misunderstand. You were very close. I'm very impressed actually." She admitted with a smile. "Keep working on it. I'm looking forward to seeing the result once you've worked out all the kinks."

Milo practically beamed then, having been praised so by such a legendary Featherstone. He embraced her briefly and gratefully.

"Thank you. I will be more careful." He promised.

"Good." Vivian replied simply. "Now, I won't keep either of you, and I really must go. It's been lovely to see you." She said by way of thanks and goodbye.

The Redwoods Rise and Fall

"Thank you again Vivian!" Clara exclaimed, pulling her into an embrace once again. "You really must come and see us again soon!"

Vivian nodded and smiled, agreeing of course, always amazed at just how quickly Clara's mood could switch from one extreme to the other.

In the back of her mind however, Vivian felt a familiar pulling drawing her away from the conversation, begging for her to leave, and it was because of that feeling that she made such a hurried goodbye.

It was an urge so deep that whenever it surfaced she struggled so much to suppress it that she'd simply given up trying, and had always eventually just allowed it to overwhelm her.

She said her goodbyes quickly and made immediately west, moving through the crowds and the buildings swiftly and with intense purpose. She smiled and waved at people as they passed and greeted her, but beneath the surface she was focused and determined, and before too long her target was in sight.

Through the open streets ahead of her appeared the view of the Redwoods in the distance, the emerging tree line flickering as she passed from street to street, her pace quickening with every fleeting step until she was almost sprinting.

Vivian passed through the western farms on the outskirts of the city, just about managing to slow her pace and her breathing and her racing heart long enough to check that nobody was watching her. Remaining as inconspicuous as possible, keeping close to the buildings and shacks along the furthest edges of the farms, Vivian checked and doubled checked that nobody could see her, for she did not want curious stragglers on her tail, for she knew that would cause upset amidst the thick forest.

Finally, satisfied that she had waited long enough, she made one final dart for the tree line, merging perfectly in amongst the ferns and trunks the second she crossed it, drifting away and disappearing totally amongst the trees, unseen and out of sight.

4

The second Vivian passed over the threshold from civilisation and into the wilderness, instantly her worries and stresses were lifted, leaving her feeling free and relaxed. She knew that whilst she was gone Archer would deal with any problems that she was not there to solve, and she always knew she could trust him to act in the people's best interests.

He had seen the work of the Greystones first hand, and Vivian knew he never wished to witness such a thing ever again, not for as long as he lived and had anything to say about it.

It was this sense of freedom that she so desired, and why the Redwoods urged her so to return at every opportunity.

For about five days and nights Vivian wandered westward. Time mattered little here amidst the trees, and the passage of the days was measured only by when she ate and when she slept.

The Redwoods were flourishing, and it always brought Vivian great joy to see them so alive and full of life and colour and sound. They offered her fruits, and she ate them gladly as she walked, brushing her hands along the tough, red bark of the trees, and running her fingers through the ferns and shrubs at her waist.

This truly was the only place and time she could forget about all that had happened, even if it was just temporarily. Whenever she reached a clearing and opened her eyes, for often she even walked by feel and sense alone rather than sight, she always envisioned Red standing before her, his head cocked to the side and his eyes loving and inquisitive.

In her mind and in her memory she would trace the steps she took to him, reach out and run her fingers through his thick, soft, warm fur, and their friendship would be renewed afresh.

Of course, this could never be so, and with that realisation, every time there came the familiar pang of pain and regret. And every time that feeling resurfaced, Vivian would once again be forced to suppress it, pushing it deeper and deeper down, hidden away for as long as she could possibly manage.

It was after those five days and nights of very nearly blissful meandering that Vivian Featherstone finally reached her destination.

Her last night's sleep had begun fitfully, but had settled somewhat during the course of the evening, as the gentle whisperings of the Redwoods all around her had quieted her racing thoughts.

So now, as the early morning sun rolled across the sky and blanketed the treetops in warm yellow rays, between the breaks in the canopy above, Vivian began to catch the first glimpses in a while of a long lost place that brought with it both good and bad memories.

Returning here always brought mixed emotions to Vivian's heart, and had done ever since she'd first visited a few months after she'd killed the Grey.

The Redwoods Rise and Fall

Featherstone Keep was a reminder of lots of things for Vivian, both of happy times, and of traumatic ones. Regardless though, she had over the years at least come to terms with those feelings, even if many of them still stirred troublesome emotions up from within the darkest depths of her heart.

She approached the old, rusted iron gates tentatively and her pulse quickened instinctively, her heart racing to a frantic rhythm in her chest, beating hastily against her ribs. The gates were slightly ajar, just as she had left them the last time she had come here, several months ago now.

Making her way up through the gates and towards the great grey Keep towering above her, Vivian surveyed the grounds critically. They were all wildly overgrown now and strewn about with the occasional littering of loose brick and rubble from the slowly crumbling structure above, not maintained in the slightest.

Vivian grimaced slightly too as her gaze swept across darkened patches of grass and earth here and there. She'd had all the bodies removed immediately upon returning here after reclaiming Virtus, both those of her family and friends, and of the Greystones. Nonetheless though, the stains of their deaths would never have been removed so easily, and those few spoiled remnants of the terrible slaughter here still remained.

The enormous heavy doors up ahead of her now were sealed tightly shut, again, just as she had left them, and she paused for a moment in their wake, on the exact spot where two of her parents had been murdered.

Sighing deeply and shaking her head, Vivian looked up at the gigantic door before her. With a single thought it creaked open effortlessly, granting her access once more to the fire-scorched and blood-blackened remnants of her old home.

Moving much more quickly, and with seemingly greater purpose now, Vivian sped through the corridors and hallways, up and down the stairwells, gliding silently across stone and wooden floors alike, knowing exactly where she was heading.

Many areas of the Keep were stained by blood and damaged by fire, left in a variety of states and in a multitude of vile colours. Other areas however, were almost entirely untouched, and at certain points on her journey to the Keep's great library, it seemed to Vivian as though nothing had ever happened here, and indeed perhaps that she had never even left.

After barely a few minutes Vivian swept through the single wooden door to the library, high up in Featherstone Keep, the wooden frame blackened and charred by flames. Sadly, the fires had in fact managed to make their way to the library, leaving many of the books and scrolls and tomes in tattered ruin.

She daren't imagine how many unique texts had been lost to the blaze, knowing of course that there was no way she would ever really know, but it had of course meant that her first few visits here had been spent almost entirely on sifting through piles of both ruined and preserved books, attempting to decipher what was in fact still vaguely readable, and what was ruined.

Hoping that once she'd found at least a few texts that were still intact, they would indeed be what she was after, Vivian had persevered.

Her search had been directed towards books that might give her a greater insight into her family's elusive, and undoubtedly eventful, past. For some reason, now that she had lost them, and come back to civilisation, Vivian wanted to know everything she possibly could about her heritage, as always her thirst for knowledge insatiable.

"That's no good…" She mumbled vaguely to herself as she flicked through a heavily bound book, moving it away to one side.

The library was lined all the way around the walls with tall bookcases bearing long, thin shelves lined with a hundred different books each. There was a large, square, wooden table right in the middle of the room, and sprawled out across it Vivian had laid piles upon piles of books, each ready and waiting to be read. These were the books she had never been able to read as a young girl, either because she had not had chance, or simply because they had not interested her.

"What about this one…" She mused, reaching across to a slightly thinner bound book, though it was still weighty enough, hefting it along the table and flicking it open.

She didn't scan through the pages for some reason with this one before opening it, and simply let it fall naturally back, splitting the pages almost directly down the middle. Immediately, Vivian's eyes lit up and she leaned forwards, pouring more intently over this one.

The crease in the book's spine told her that it had been opened to these pages a goodly number of times in the past, hence why it had naturally fallen there.

It was a family tree, outlining the Featherstone bloodline as far back even as ten generations. Vivian bent closely over the text and swallowed hard, her eyes flitting over the names swiftly and eagerly.

Her name was at the bottom, and above it were her parents' names. And then above her father's name were two more names, his mother and father, Arianne and Richard Featherstone, and so on and so forth. The line continued up the page in what seemed to be a single, strong and unbroken strand, with each couple having birthed seemingly only one child.

That was a strange concept to Vivian, but the more she thought about it, the more she supposed it made sense, and that perhaps, unknowingly, by some force beyond their control, the Featherstone bloodline had been kept in such a way as to preserve it, but then also so as not to allow its power to spread too widely.

It all felt very specific, and ultimately purpose-driven, and sent something of a shiver cascading down Vivian's spine. The thought that her life was not in her control even in the slightest was not an alien one, for she had pondered the notion many times, but nonetheless, that didn't make the idea any less unnerving.

All those times she had so narrowly escaped death, and all the things she had done that were so impossible and so implausible; it seemed in that moment of revelation that there was no way any of it could have been avoided.

Her mind wandered for a minute to what might still remain in store for her, for she was obviously still alive, and so surely there was still more for her to do.

Pushing those complicated and brain numbing thoughts clearly aside, Vivian focused again on her task at hand, delving once more back to the book she held so firmly in her grasp, flicking the page over lightly with her thumb.

On the next page there was no diagram or family tree, but instead a long, thin column of scrawled text that seemed to have been written rather hastily, down the left hand side of the page.

It seemed to her a strange way to write, and was completely different to anything she had seen before in any of the other books, which only funnelled her interest in this particular tome evermore greatly.

And it was with deep sorrow that William Featherstone raised his almighty hand and brought great change to the world, for such an act is never undertaken lightly.

His choice however was none, for the world beyond the boundaries of man needed protection greater than that which the Featherstone's alone could provide. He bore the responsibility of his task without hesitation, and his will was done.

Ross Turner

*The blood of the great forests was
immediately changed, and indeed
so was the blood of the animals.*

Vivian paused for a moment and lifted her
eyes from the text, breathing deeply as she did so,
realising she'd been holding her breath. She
remembered then words her father had once said to
her, in a story, about the blood of the trees and of the
animals.

She thumbed backwards a page and checked
the family tree. William Featherstone was indeed on
there, nine generations above her. Clearly that story
had been passed down without fail from generation to
generation.

'But when the forests turned red, the blood of
the trees changed, and so did the blood of the
animals…' Her father had told her once, long ago.
His words rang in her ears still. 'And when the blood
of the animals changed, all sorts of things changed
with it…'

She remembered it as if he had told her just
yesterday, clear as day.

Knowledge of this book however, that Vivian
now held so firmly in her grasp, had not been passed
down to her along with the story. She imagined it
probably had been to her parents, and to their parents
before them. She knew in her heart that her parents
would have told her when the time was right. It had
just so happened that their time had been taken from
them.

Regardless though, she had discovered it on
her own, and Vivian somehow guessed that she

wouldn't have been allowed to evade it, even if she had tried.

She turned her heavy eyes back to the text.

And with that change came many new things. The newfound Redwood Forest and all of its life evolved so quickly, and in such a manner, that their power and knowledge was unmatched.

The spirit of the woodlands lived within each animal and creature that it protected, and so it learned and grew with each new life, only amplifying its evolution and wisdom.

That had to be the voice of the Redwoods, surely, Vivian thought to herself. She cast her mind back over all the times she had listened to their words, both when she had lived with Red and Clover, and then also after their deaths, and how she had always marvelled at the Redwood's seemingly infinite knowledge and wisdom and patience.

She cast her eyes back down once more, now almost at the bottom of the page, and it looked as though this strange column of scrawl continued on for a goodly few more pages after this one.

And the greatest of all the changes came to those fearsome beasts to

*the south, for their power even
before William Featherstone had
raised his hand, was unrivalled by
any other. This new power brought
to them...*

A sudden bang in the distance snatched away Vivian's attention, and she snapped her head sharply over her shoulder, eyes locking on the entrance to the library. The echoing sound of the slamming door in the distance reverberated in through the door to the library, slightly ajar. The sound rang in her ears where she sat like a warning siren.

She sprung to her feet and shot across the room, all in one fluid motion, her movements practiced and precise, even predatory.

Her heart raced and she pressed herself as close to the wall as she could, her breathing fast and shallow and anxious. A pit had formed in her stomach, and she even felt a little sick.

Peering around the door, Vivian glanced up and down the stone walkway of the corridor outside for as far as she could see. But there was nothing to be seen, and all remained silent.

Holding perfectly still for a few more minutes, breathing only short shallow breaths, and only when she dared, Vivian closed her eyes and cast a wandering thought out over the Keep.

It was but a matter of seconds however before her concentration was interrupted by another bang, this one much closer than the first, and the hollow, echoing sound of long, heavy footsteps, bouncing their way through the hallways of her old home.

That was it.

There was someone here.

And they were close.

Vivian stole away from the library on silent feet, keeping close to the walls and peering round doorways and sharp turns in the hallways before taking them, heading always in the direction that the sounds had come from.

The footsteps continued to ring in her ears, yet seemed to come from all around her, the walls reverberating the sounds back and forth amidst the silence so much that she began to wonder whether she was in fact moving towards the origin of the footsteps or away from it.

Eventually, after creeping down another flight of stairs and peering round to scan the next corridor ahead of her, craning her neck, Vivian caught a glimpse of a flickering shadow just moving out of sight, right at the end of the hallway.

Her heart surged with strange exhilaration afresh and she sprinted silently after the intruder. There were windows set in this corridor and the afternoon light streamed in, blinding Vivian in brief second-long flashes as she passed quickly by each one.

She careered round the corner at the end, not bothering to stop and peek first, and ground to a furious and resolute halt. She gasped deeply and locked her eyes forward, training them on the man standing before her, his gaze in turn focused on her, at the other end of the corridor.

It was as if he'd known she would come.

The stranger stood with a wide, powerful stance. His shoulders were broad and the skin on his face and hands was fair, though yet still weathered, clearly from a life of some kind of labour. A small, brown satchel was slung over his one shoulder that looked light enough to carry only bare essentials.

Most curious of all however, Vivian noticed, even in that briefest first glance, was that beneath his sandy brown hair, there was a very unusual look about his face, for his features were most uncommon, yet they were also strangely familiar to her. And upon his unique features, chiselled and well angled, he wore an expression of surprise and awe and curiosity, all combined into one.

They stood there for barely a second or two, and in that time Vivian took all of this in and more, right from his well-worn and ragged tanned leather clothes, to his deepest of expressions.

And in turn again, he too took in a vast amount about her.

He marvelled at her beauty, regardless of the fact that it had been haggard by time and burdens alike, and too at her clothes, so simple and plain for one of such fabled power.

Vivian opened her mouth involuntarily to speak, not knowing what to say, indeed captivated by the man before her. But before she had chance to gather her thoughts, shape her tongue and form her words, he exploded into movement and darted out of sight, sprinting away down the next corridor.

That snapped Vivian back into focus.

"HEY!" She yelled after him, settling for something easy and with only a single syllable.

And, of course, she immediately took off in pursuit, hurtling down the hallway and round the corner at the end, following both the sound of his heavy footsteps and the fleeting glimpses she caught of him each time she careered round a corner.

Finally they were on the ground floor and Vivian's heart was racing. She was neither gaining nor losing pace on the intruder, and she kept attempting to gather her will, but with each attempt she made, for some reason, her focus fell flat, and so she simply kept up the chase.

That was all she could do.

The stranger burst from the heavy front door to the Keep and leapt down towards the iron gates, his movements easy and athletic, not once even breaking his stride. He swept quickly down towards the treeline and had almost even disappeared amongst the vast red trunks before Vivian too bounded out into the streaming sunlight.

"WAIT!" She shrieked as she tore down after him.

But of course he didn't, and he slipped and darted into the trees and disappeared in an instant.

Vivian charged after him, racing as fast as her beating heart to keep pace with the man who had disturbed her.

Who was he?

What in the world was he doing here?

What had he been looking for?

Why did she feel like she'd seen him before?

Vivian's thoughts raced through her mind faster even than her legs churned, and she tore through the open iron gates and into the comparable dark of the woodlands to pursue the answers she so desired.

5

Branches whipped at Vivian's face as she ran, darting round and through and beneath bushes and shrubs, desperately trying to keep the man she was pursuing in sight, yet every time losing him amongst the trees.

For what seemed like hours Vivian pursued the stranger that she felt as though she recognised, chasing after him through the endless woodlands, tinted with such an ancient red that it was very much a part of the makeup of the world itself.

The Redwoods didn't speak to her as she ran, and even if they had done, she likely wouldn't have been able to focus enough to hear them. Instead though, as she hurried forward, whenever Vivian lost sight of her stranger, she gained a certain sense from the trees all around her as to whether she was still on his trail or not, directed almost entirely by her and their senses combined.

Eventually, each time, she always emerged into a clearing of some kind and caught sight of her target once again, resuming her chase.

Though it had at first seemed that this man's stamina was endless, he was at last proving at least that he was human, and his pace was slowing.

Vivian however, though of course she was still human, could force her body to continue without slowing, feeding her muscles and her lungs and heart with her sometimes seemingly infinite power. This meant, essentially, that she could run for as long as her power lasted, and with power as vast and extensive as hers, that could truly prove to be rather a long time.

"HEY!" She yelled again, gaining on the stranger with every step. He threw a quick and clearly exhausted glance over his shoulder, his eyes widening as they laid their sights briefly upon Vivian.

The image he found was of his pursuer, not looking even slightly wearied, replenished to a point that seemed both entirely inhuman and impossible, and the sight shocked him beyond belief.

Soon enough, he was able to outrun her no more. Forced to stop with cramping muscles, a heaving chest and gasping breaths, the stranger backed up to the thick trunk of a tree, holding his hands up defensively, but so out of breath unable to speak.

Vivian wasted no time, having let him evade her once already.

An invisible force knocked what little wind there was in the stranger's lungs from him, and he was pinned back up against the tree, unable to move, dragged four or five feet up from the ground.

"Wha…?" Was all he managed to gasp as his body was restrained, and all that remained of his breath was stolen.

"Right then…" Vivian stated, placing her hands on her hips and walking right up to the man pinned against the tree by her invisible force. She was not even short of breath, let alone struggling to breathe as he was, and though she was wearied and fatigued from her efforts, of course she did not let that show.

Looking at him more closely now, and in better light, Vivian could see that he was about her age, and his unusual features made him actually very handsome, though that wasn't what concerned her right at that moment.

"Who the hell are you!?" She demanded, the frustration and even tinted anger in her voice all too clear.

He wheezed and puffed for breath again, unable to reply, still held in Vivian's invisible and suffocating grasp. She relaxed her tension slightly, allowing him to breathe gratefully, and he caught his breath for a minute or two before he was eventually able to reply, returning Vivian's fierce gaze with one of innocence and strange curiosity.

"My name is Kael." He eventually managed to respond. Speaking simply and matter-of-factly, his voice soft, though it had a definite edge to it: the kind of sharp and astute tone developed through hardship.

Vivian knew it well.

"Kael?" She questioned, raising an eyebrow. She had never heard the name before, and it sounded strange to her.

"Yes…" He replied uncertainly, as if he'd somehow wronged her by having the incorrect name.

"Where are you from?" Vivian demanded, her voice firm. "I've never heard that name before."

"I'm from the north." He replied, as if that explained everything without the need for any further elaboration.

"The north?" Vivian questioned. "What do you mean, the north?"

"I'm from the north." He repeated, as if he didn't quite grasp what she was asking of him. "Up past the great plains. Beyond the northern border of the Redwood Empire." He expanded.

"Beyond the Redwoods?" Vivian asked then, her voice opening and the harshness dropping from it almost completely, as if what he was suggesting was utterly ludicrous.

"Yes…" He replied carefully, again unsure what he'd done wrong - apparently just by revealing his name and where he was from he had baffled his pursuer.

Nothing was said then for a minute or two, and a bizarre silence hung between the two of them, like a connection that was long overdue reunifying. Finally, Kael decided to break the quiet, for even the whisperings in the trees above them had ceased.

"Vivian, right?" He asked, his tone admittedly a little uncertain. "Vivian Featherstone?"

His question however, did nothing to stir Vivian's tongue, and the sheer fact that he seemed to know exactly who she was, although he wasn't even from the Redwood Empire, shocked her some.

How…?" She started, looking for the right words of accusation, though she wasn't entirely sure what she was accusing him of.

"You come out here quite often…" Kael continued. "Nowhere near as much as you used to though…"

Suddenly Vivian forced him further up the tree and the choking clasp around his neck tightened. He gasped desperately for breath and clawed at the restraints around his neck and body, but there were none to be found, and he simply continued to struggle.

"How do you know me!?" Vivian demanded, hissing her words fiercely through gritted teeth.

It wasn't too much of a surprise that he knew who she was, most did. But the fact that he knew about her regular visits to Featherstone Keep usurped Vivian's calm somewhat.

"Please!" Kael managed to gasp between weak and desperate gulps for air. "I can't…I can't breathe!"

"Tell me!" Vivian ordered him, a red shade covering her view of the poor, innocent soul she was crushing beneath her will.

Finally, after another thirty seconds or so, Kael's struggles began to weaken, and his kicking legs hung more limply. Vivian suddenly panicked, realising all of a sudden in that moment that she was killing this man, for no reason other than that she'd lost control of herself.

Shame swept over her in an enormous flurrying wave, and Vivian immediately released the stranger Kael completely.

He dropped to the ground with a heavy thud and took deep, grateful gulps of air, able to finally fill his lungs freely. His recovery took a few long minutes, and Vivian took several steps back to give him space, feeling decidedly ashamed of herself.

Eventually Kael looked up, a strange expression set on his face, and he sat back against the tree he had only minutes ago been pinned to, looking up at Vivian openly, and his face entirely unreadable to her.

If she could have described it as anything, the word that came to mind would have been, for some strange reason, affectionate.

"I'm sorry…" She admitted, her voice quiet and filled with apologetic shame.

"Not to worry." He replied, brushing his scrape with death off somewhat casually. "No harm done. I probably should have explained myself first." He admitted honestly. "That probably sounded like I've been stalking you, which, considering the stories I've heard flying round, I can imagine isn't the most comforting thing…"

Vivian nodded slowly in agreement, but said nothing, silently urging him to continue.

High above them the white blanket of clouds circled endlessly, growing and gathering together into darker and darker bundles by the hour. By now they had blocked the sun entirely and the air felt heavy, clearly thick with the preparing onslaught of a storm.

"The place where I used to live, where I was born…" Kael began, his thoughts clearly lost to the past as he recalled it to the forefront of his mind.

A pained look crossed his face that Vivian recognised all too well, and her features softened noticeably, having something of an inkling of what might be coming next.

"It was far to the north, like I said, past the edge of the Redwoods and the plains. It was a place called Hope." He explained. "We raised cattle and farmed the land, trying to grow enough food for ourselves, and then also to sell so that we could pay our Lord."

He paused for a moment, as if he was going to say something else, but instead changed his mind, deciding against it, and flitted back to his tale.

"There was a terrible drought. We have no idea what caused it, but it brought us hard times. Our animals all grew weak and eventually died, our crops withered, and we struggled more and more to revive the land every year. We had no money to go anywhere, and though we pleaded to our Lord for help, he never listened to us."

Vivian's heart began to throb as she thought of those who farmed the land around the outskirts of Virtus, and how she had spent years considering their every need, along with all her other people. It sounded as though Kael's Lord had not been bound by such principles.

"After another six months, since we hadn't been able to pay our rent, our Lord eventually drove us off of his land, though I doubt since then he's been able to find anyone to replace us, unless the rains have returned…" Kael continued. "Without food and shelter, it wasn't long before we got desperate. But there was nothing we could do…"

He sighed deeply and his expression saddened, though it was still difficult to read.

"I was the only one still strong enough to travel, but it didn't matter. There wasn't any food around. My father told me to go south to escape the drought. He told me about the Redwoods and that they were protected. He said there would always be food there. So I left…" His voice dropped and Vivian didn't need to hear any more.

She felt suddenly a strong connection between herself and Kael then. It was a link forged by the similarities between them. She too had abandoned her family, not by choice, but out of necessity: simply to survive.

"I didn't know anything about the Redwood Empire." Kael admitted. "I'd heard stories sure, but they were just stories to me. I knew nothing about the feud between the Greystones and your family, at least not until I eventually reached Virtus."

"What have you heard?" Vivian asked then, curious to know what he knew of her family's tragedy, being, quite possibly, one of the only people to now live in Virtus who hadn't suffered the Greystone's rule.

He shrugged slightly as if he'd heard many different versions of the same tale.

"That the Greystone's had always hated the Featherstones. That they weren't powerful enough to overrule them, so they tried to kill them. But you survived, and eventually came back to kill them all."

Vivian nodded for a moment, considering his words.

"That's pretty much what happened." She admitted. "In the simplest terms anyway. So how do you know so much about me?" She questioned.

"It's quite simple really…" Kael started, smirking slightly, though Vivian wasn't quite sure why. "I work as a farmhand on one of the farms on the western edge of Virtus. They were looking for someone to work the fields, and I have a lot of experience in that sort of thing. I was working the fields in Hope pretty much from the day I could walk."

Vivian considered that, but didn't say anything of it. It sounded as though Kael's upbringing had been a tough one.

"I think anyone in Virtus could point you out leagues away. And you've come and gone into the Redwoods there ever since I arrived here." He continued.

"I didn't think anyone had seen me leave." Vivian admitted honestly, realising that perhaps she hadn't been as careful as she'd thought.

"I've been doing my best to fit since the first day I got here." He explained. "I've made it my business to fit in: to keep my head down. I'm not surprised you haven't noticed me." He paused for a moment, a smile touching his lips. "You're very hard to ignore though…" He finally added, his smile turning into an affectionate smirk that flashed across his face again, but once more, Vivian missed its meaning.

He'd actually caught her very off guard now, she realised. He'd seen her come and go probably almost every time she'd come to visit the Keep, and she hadn't once noticed him, even though his features were so different and so unique compared to anyone's she'd ever seen, that they practically jumped out and slapped her across the face.

For some reason then she felt guilty for never having noticed him.

Nonetheless, she certainly had done now.

"Why did you follow me?" She asked, trying to collect her thoughts and rationalise them. "If you've seen me come and go so many times, why now?"

"At first I had no idea where you were going." He replied with another shrug. "But then the more stories I heard and the more I thought about it, it only made sense that you were going to visit your old home." He reasoned aloud. "Eventually I just grew too curious to ignore it any longer." He admitted openly and with a light hearted laugh. "And, if I'm perfectly honest, I desperately wanted to meet you."

Vivian didn't know how to respond to that, and her heart jumped into her mouth for a moment.

Though she had faltered slightly, she at least understood a little, both about the pain of leaving his family, and about his burning curiosity, for those two things she had experienced herself, many a time.

What she did not understand, however, was his apparent desire to meet her, without needing something.

The thought was simply alien to her.

For years Vivian had been her people's first port of call for problems and issues. And now, this stranger from another land, whom she had apparently overlooked a hundred times, wanted to meet her because…

She eventually realised, after a few more minutes of silent deliberation, that she didn't in fact have any idea why he'd wanted to meet her, and her heart pounded heavily against her ribs at that thought, stirring emotions that she had long forgotten, or perhaps never even awoken.

As much as she might have wanted to pursue that line of questioning however, and Kael could see her mind churning, Vivian decided instead to avert her burning curiosity, for perhaps the first time in her life, and asked instead a different question.

"Have you had trouble with the cattle on your farm?" She asked, seemingly out of the blue, and Kael smiled knowingly, but said nothing else of it.

"Trouble with the cattle?" He repeated. "What do you mean?"

"I heard some of the farms are having problems with something killing their cattle." She expanded, realising how vague her first question had been.

"No." He replied simply. "We haven't had any problems. I've heard of problems in the south though." He commented. "The man who owns the farm I work on, his name is Linton. He's a good man. His cousin owns a farm in the south. I think they've had some problems with something killing their cattle…"

"I see…" Vivian replied, not really knowing what else to say. "I'm going to have to go and find out what's going on…" She continued, but her voice trailed off and left her sentence unfinished, as her eyes wandered past Kael's face for the first time since their conversation had begun.

They widened as she noticed what had happened around them, without them noticing, and Vivian's sudden realisation forced Kael to tear his gaze from her also. He too looked all about then, shock and uncertainty gripping him, and admittedly quite afraid.

Unbeknownst to them, as they had been talking, they'd been so engrossed by each other that they hadn't noticed their audience forming around them, watching their every move, and focusing on their words intently.

Around them, huddled in a circle about the clearing within which they'd been talking, a hundred and more animals had gathered, their eyes and ears turned intently towards the couple. Deer and squirrels and rabbits and hedgehogs and even wolves and bears alike.

Their expressions were strange: curious and intent, and even expectant, though what they were hopeful of, Vivian hadn't a clue.

She closed her eyes and listened to the whisperings around them for a moment then, wondering what in the world was happening.

What were the Redwoods trying to tell her?

Nonetheless though, as hard as she tried to listen, they remained silent still, giving her nothing. It seemed that these animals, all the hundreds of them, the deer and rabbits and foxes and wolves and bears, had all gathered for something, but what it was, Vivian was not to know.

They all stood there for a moment, the animals and Kael and Vivian alike, staring at each other.

Eventually, not knowing what else to do, Vivian took a careful and hesitant step towards them.

Immediately they all scattered, darting into movement as if something had startled them terribly, and they all bounded off in every direction, melting away amidst the trees and shrubs as if they had never been disturbed.

6

Their journey back eastward to Virtus took much less time than Vivian's original journey out to the Keep. Her pace was not the sauntering amble that she had adopted whilst walking alone, but instead a more focused and steady speed that spoke of purpose and time constraints.

Admittedly, aside from the thundering rainstorm that struck them, much of that was due to the fact that, especially at first, she felt uneasy in Kael's company. Not because he was difficult to get along with, for in fact he was very easy going and polite, but simply because she was not used to travelling with anyone.

The only time she had ever done so had been a long while ago, and even then her company had come in the form of a great red bear, not a handsome and mysterious stranger from a land far to the north.

Perhaps the hardest thing about the journey however, was not growing used to the company that Kael provided, for that happened very easily, and in fact almost instantly. Instead, it was attempting to avert her eyes from him as they walked and as they rested, and even as they ate and bedded down for the night.

It happened more and more as the days passed, and Vivian found it increasingly difficult to avoid glancing over at her companion at virtually every opportunity. Embarrassingly though, quite often as she did so, she found that he was doing exactly the same thing, and every time seemingly without fail they caught each other's gazes.

For a brief moment they would be locked there, before Vivian tore her eyes away, blushing furiously.

What was happening?

What was she doing?

Vivian berated herself furiously with every thwarted glance, but nonetheless, regardless of how many times they caught each other, they still continued to do it, for just as neither of them knew why they were doing it, equally they could find no reason to stop.

Eventually though, after a few days, the mass of trees around them gradually began to thin, and the view ahead of them slowly transformed from a sea of red to a flurry of rising buildings, mills and stores and homes alike, all surrounded by an array of sown and planted and fallow fields.

It was almost noon as they broke through the tree line on the outskirts of Virtus, emerging from the woods unseen, skirting their way over to the first building they could reach, running shyly as if they'd done something wrong.

Having not eaten that morning, Vivian's stomach was growling fiercely, telling her that indeed it was time she found food. It had been a long time since she and Red had been running starving through the Redwoods, and her stomach had grown accustomed to being filled much more regularly than that.

Kael made no move to leave her and return to his farmstead, and to be perfectly honest, for some reason, Vivian didn't want him to, so she didn't dare question it.

Instead, they headed immediately for the nearest tavern, their stomachs commanding them and their noses guiding them.

From outside, the inn looked as though it had been built at the beginning of days, for its stone walls were crumbling at every opportunity, leaving them mottled with the marks of time, having somehow even withstood the Greystone's awful rule.

The inside however, was in much better condition, and had clearly been well cared for. The owners were a small family of a mother, father and son, and it was obvious that they knew their livelihood depended on bringing their customers back in, day after day, week after week.

Wooden stools and tall tables arranged up and down the length of the tavern were lit with well-stocked oil lamps, and the place was both unusually and scrupulously clean and tidy. The food they served was not even the tiniest bit stale, and it was clear the owners knew exactly how to bring their patrons flooding back, for the long thin room lined with tables and chairs and stools, all running parallel to the bar, was practically heaving.

Luckily, all that hustle and bustle allowed Vivian and Kael to slip in relatively unnoticed, although of course there were some who spied the virtus of the People as she entered, they respected the fact that she was likely just here to be fed like the rest of them, and, thankfully, didn't highlight her arrival to the whole tavern.

Within minutes Vivian and Kael were seated, and had placed before them steaming bowls of soup and thick chunks of sliced bread, still warm from the oven. They delved straight in and devoured their meals without a moment's hesitation.

Partway through, once her hunger had been somewhat satisfied, Vivian turned half of her attention to the others all around them, each tucking into their own meals or diving into their tankards.

"My hams are the best in the city..." One man boasted to another, apparently having come here for business, or perhaps simply to gloat.

"And she rebuilt my house right before my eyes..." Another man told his audience. "An incredible thing it was. She lifted everything into the air and slotted it all together..."

Vivian smiled slyly and turned her attention elsewhere again, eventually finding the conversation she'd been searching for. She'd learned quite some time ago now that if there was news to be had, and stories to be told, taverns were usually the best place to hear them.

"Terrible it is." A much more elderly man said to another then, a little ways behind Vivian and Kael on a small, round table. "Whatever it is that's been attacking the livestock, it hasn't stopped. Cows, sheep, chickens, it doesn't seem to matter."

Kael saw Vivian listening intently to the man's words and attuned his ears also, picking up the conversation, presumably about the southern farms.

"Always on the nights of the attacks, you can hear great terrible roars and howls coming from the Redwoods, all mixed up in the darkness. It makes the cattle very skittish I can imagine. It's like they know something's coming for them, and with bloody good reason. Come morning, they've lost one, two, three, sometimes even five or six at a time. Blood everywhere."

"Can't the owner lock them in the barn or something?" One of the men in his audience asked. "Surely if he kept them hidden away…"

"He tried that." The elderly man replied with a dramatic sigh, clearly enjoying his storytelling. "He even posted watchmen outside the barn armed with crossbows and swords. But the same thing just kept on happening, only worse. Come morning, the barn was ripped to shreds, the cattle had been taken again, and the watchmen had disappeared."

That was it.

Vivian had heard enough already, and she was far too duty bound to simply stand by idly.

It was one thing to have a few sheep go missing, but this was something else entirely. She would not stand for this, whatever it was, attacking her people, killing them and ruining their livelihoods, it had to be stopped.

She rose purposefully to her feet, with Kael in tow, and marched directly over to the old man who had been telling the news.

"My good sir…" She greeted him. He immediately recognised her of course, and bowed his head respectfully, his tongue stammering for words.

"Oh my…Miss Featherstone…" He stuttered. "What an honour…"

By now all heads in the tavern had turned their way, and Vivian's presence was no longer inconspicuous, not by any stretch of the imagination.

"Don't worry about that..." She replied, waving his courtesies aside with a gesture of her hand. "Please, forgive me, was that the southern farms you were describing just? I've heard there have been problems..." She asked of him.

"Yes my Lady." He responded automatically. Vivian was of course not royalty, but many of her people still treated her as though she was. She, however, was not overly fond of the pleasantries, and much preferred to just get straight to the point.

"Which ones?" She asked more specifically.

"I believe the particular farm I described is owned by a man named Jared."

"Jared?" Vivian repeated, though she had to admit the name didn't ring any bells. It would have been virtually impossible for her to know everyone in the city.

"Yes. He owns one of the southernmost farms, right on the edge of the Redwoods..."

"Thank you." Vivian replied gratefully. "These attacks you described, are they all true?" She asked.

"To the last word." The old man vowed.

"Very well then." Vivian said resolutely. "I shall travel south and see to the problem myself. It's not something that I wish to hear is continuing."

"Jared will be in your debt." The elderly man replied with another bow of his head. "And I think his men will all sleep more soundly at night knowing you are there to protect them."

"Please could you send word that I'll be down to aid them?" Vivian requested.

"I will carry the message myself." He replied, rising from his seat as he spoke.

"Very well. Thank you." Vivian concluded. "I will see to it that this threat, whatever it is, is stopped once and for all."

It was well into the afternoon, and a few clouds dotted lazily above cast huge shadows over the city here and there, blocking the sunlight in great, billowing masses, as Vivian strode briskly through the streets. Whilst it was not cold, a swift, chill breeze certainly took all warmth out of the day, and it was clear that the seasons were turning rapidly.

Vivian pulled her cloak more tightly up around her neck as she headed back home, escorted still by Kael.

He had insisted on walking her all the way home, having come this far and not wanting to leave her to make the rest of the way alone. She had briefly argued that it wasn't necessary, which of course they both knew was the case. But nonetheless, they didn't want to part ways quite yet, and so she hadn't pushed the matter too hard, and he hadn't budged on his insistence.

As a matter of fact, Vivian was growing to very much enjoy Kael's company, and even perhaps, just perhaps, to see him as, and to trust him more, than a simple acquaintance or passer-by in her life.

She had, for obvious reasons, after she'd defeated the Greystones, found it very hard to trust and to love, because those feelings always opened doorways to pain, both from the past, and potentially for the future. Vivian had spent the most recent years of her life, and even many before that, running from that very same anguish, and was not eager to welcome it back afresh.

It was only now though, as they were walking back towards her house, right through the centre of the city, that Vivian realised just how different Kael was to those others all around them.

His skin tone, his body shape, and even the way he held himself. He had done exceptionally well to keep such a low profile.

Now, to Vivian, her eyes opened to his presence, he stood out leagues from the rest.

She even began to wonder exactly how in the world, having passed by those western farms so many times, she had not noticed him, when he had so clearly always noticed her.

That same, strange feeling that she had felt before in the Redwoods began to creep back into residence within her once more then, not so much stirring and awakening this time, but instead reigniting with a fierce and unbelievable flame. Her heart jumped and skipped a few beats, her temperature rose, and her breath quickened, though she desperately tried to hide all of these things.

Kael seemed not to notice, but if Vivian had learned anything about the young man over the past few days, it was that he was not so easily fooled as that.

Whatever was happening to her, Vivian couldn't believe how different it was to anything she'd ever felt before, and those incredible and overwhelming new emotions rose to the surface uncontrollably, pouring out and filling her fragile heart with an exciting and newfound hope.

7

Finally, a few hours later, Vivian and Kael reached her small, run down house in the centre of the city. Admittedly, though he didn't quite understand why, Kael found it strange that in the whole time they'd spent together leading up to that moment, Vivian had never once referred to this place as her home. Instead, she had only ever called it her house: the place in which she stayed, but did not live.

After all, home is where the heart is, and Vivian's had perhaps been lost long ago.

But then again, perhaps not.

There was no time for respite however, for the moment they arrived, Archer immediately came bustling out, obviously having been watching and waiting for Vivian's arrival.

"It's about bloody time you got back!" He instantly remarked, his voice tinged with more than a little annoyance. "Where in the world have you been!? Do you have any idea at all how much to do you left me to deal with!?"

His voice rose and dropped in great swells and crescendos as he berated her.

"Any idea AT ALL!?" He finally ended with, having to stop to catch his breath, save he might have passed out.

Vivian was struggling to listen however, for something about the distant look in Kael's eyes tugged at the delicate strings of her freshly awakened emotions.

"You can't keep just disappearing and relying on me to do everything!" Archer continued his rant, apparently unaware that Vivian wasn't focused in the slightest. "You need to have a system in place to help deal with all these things!"

It wasn't just a great distance that Vivian saw in Kael, but it was pain also. He glanced at her briefly, unable to keep his eyes away any longer, and then Vivian knew. She knew that now, finally, after being thrown together, so out of the blue, Kael was going to leave.

A tight pull in her chest begged her to stop him, but her lips would not move.

"I can see you have much to do…" He said solemnly. "I don't wish to intrude. I'm pleased to have escorted you home safely…"

Though he spoke, and though his words were sincere, they were empty of the truth, for they said both everything and nothing of what the young man really wanted to tell her, and indeed also of what young Vivian wanted to hear.

They were a mere formality, for Archer's sake, and were like stones in Kael's heart as he spoke them.

"I was wondering who you were!" Archer exclaimed then. "You could have got her to hurry up a bit!" He grumbled, obviously missing the emotion that was passing between them in that moment.

"I…I…" Vivian stammered, but that was all she managed, for the words simply would not come to her.

She had never been so dumbfounded in all her life.

Ross Turner

"It was lovely to finally meet you." Kael admitted honestly, smiling affectionately and looking at Vivian in a way that told her, for some reason, that he cared for her so deeply that he simply could not describe it.

It was a look she hadn't seen for years, not since Red had died.

And so, when Kael finally thanked her for her company and bid her his final farewell, it was with great longing that Vivian watched him slowly walk away. He vanished amongst the crowds in the distance, looking back only once, his eyes full of longing, leaving a whole new feeling of emptiness to open up inside of her.

The rest of Vivian's day, her whole week in fact, was devoted entirely to the matters of business that she had missed during her absence. Archer made sure of it.

Though many aspects of the city ran themselves: small businesses and local trade and such. It was when these things encountered problems, much of the time spanning from something as simple as a minor disagreement, to a major crisis, that Vivian was consulted.

Having spent their years under the Greystone rule being told solely what to do, or perhaps more accurately what not to do, the people had grown away from using their own initiative, in simple fear of being punished for doing so. Therefore, the vast majority of all problems, even still, were brought to Vivian's doorstep to resolve.

70

Many of them simply required logic and fairness to work through, where perhaps land needed to be divided, or where goods and profits needed to be split equally between parties.

Others required a slightly more tactful approach, for some of those nobles who had been more favoured under the Greystone rule had gained wealth during that time, whilst others had lost it. Now, such favouritism was no more, for Vivian had no time for it, and so some of them simply needed bringing back down to size.

All in all, whilst each task in of itself was not overly taxing, combined, the sheer volume of issues was overwhelming. Though he may have moaned and grumbled about it, Vivian had to admit that Archer had a point. She would not be able to leave again without setting some sort of system in place to deal with this.

In fact, if she was totally honest, she could have done with one while she was there too.

It was three days after she had arrived back, and since Kael had left, that Vivian received a message from Jared, the owner of the farm that had seemingly been under attack. His message thanked her in advance for her assistance, but she couldn't help but note a certain urgency and desperation in its writing, and knew she was running out of time.

She decided then she would simply have to take a chance. It might work, it might not, but realistically, she'd been left with little other option.

Vivian then set about recruiting her closest friends in the city, and when she thought of turning to friends, she meant of course turning to those who had assisted and advised her the most over the past few years, offering her invaluable help and aid.

Selecting only those who had offered in the past to help her voluntarily, she swiftly and efficiently separated the willing from the unwilling, and soon rallied her numbers. Not only did she choose just those who had assisted her in the past, but she made sure to select men and women from very different backgrounds: farming, business, stonework, and even past poachers, to ensure that their view of whatever problems were presented to them was as wide and all-encompassing as physically possible.

These few select men and women, numbering only seven in total, became the first trial for her new House.

All the while though, even as Vivian worked and rallied and planned, preparing those she had recruited for the task ahead of them, whilst still somehow dealing with it all herself, she thought of Kael. In every spare moment, and sometimes even when she was supposed to be otherwise occupied with thought, her mind wandered to the image of his face in her mind. She was simply unable to forget that final look he'd cast her before he'd left, and every time she remembered it, the sight in her mind's eye brought fresh emotion to her, all over again.

Thankfully, since her return, up until that point, Vivian had managed to somehow elude her nightmares, and had slept rather peacefully. Occasionally she had dreamt in fleeting images of Kael, but for the most part her dreams had been filled with the blissful silence of nothing in particular.

The Redwoods Rise and Fall

Five days after her return however, once things with her new system had begun to settle, Vivian suffered the dread of her night terrors once more, and, seemingly out of the blue, she found herself faced with one she hadn't suffered for a long while.

Stood back in the library of Featherstone Keep, a whistling wind whipping through the corridors, Vivian shivered violently against the cold seeping through to her bones. The temperature was chilling, and her breath steamed out in front of her face in great wisps of cloud.

All about her, strewn across the large, square table and across the floor, were mountains of books, all torn and ripped and burned, discarded everywhere she looked.

Glancing up, her mouth dropping open in horror, Vivian saw that the walls of the room were all smeared and streaked blood red.

Then her hands suddenly felt sticky and rough. She looked down again, only this time to be disgusted at what she saw.

She too was covered in blood, and in her stained hands she held the blade that had spilled all of this pain and anguish. The knife was small and its edge was nicked a hundred and more times, damaged by the countless bones it had split in its lifetime.

Vivian dropped the blade with a sharp breath and fled from the scene, stumbling over the piles of books all around her as she did so. Bursting out into the corridor she shivered again and rubbed her bare arms with her hands, for out here it was even colder.

The lit torches spaced evenly out along the walls stretched away in both directions all the way down the corridor. Then, to her right, the long line of torches slowly began to extinguish, darkening the hallway at the far end. Closer and closer the darkness drew as the torches were one by one snuffed out.

She fled that too, tearing away and running full pelt in the other direction, desperately hoping that she could somehow escape. Her bare feet stung on the freezing floor as she ran, and her hands left bloodied prints and she careered round every corner uncontrollably.

Then, suddenly, as she rounded perhaps the fifth corner, she collided full pelt with a man who had been stood just out of view. The wind was knocked from her and Vivian sprawled to the floor with a cry, grazing her knees and elbows on the hard, unforgiving stone.

Catching her breath and looking up, she immediately wished she hadn't.

It was the Grey, unchanged entirely from when she had killed him all those years ago.

For a time they simply held each other's gaze, as Vivian rose slowly to her feet. They were locked together, neither of them able to move, both knowing that what was about to happen, that what had already happened was about to be repeated.

From seemingly nowhere, Vivian had her blade in her hand once again, and she raised it slowly and purposefully, knowing exactly what she was going to do.

The Grey seemed not to care, as if he'd accepted his fate already, and that no matter how many times Vivian killed him, it would make no difference. He would still be able to haunt her until the end of her days, and she could never rob him of that power over her.

She screamed then, wildly and savagely, lunging forward with all the speed and strength she could muster, driving the blade forwards and straight towards his heart.

Vivian awoke with a heavy jolt and let loose the same animalistic shriek that she had done in her nightmare. Her heart raced and pounded like a heavy drum against her ribs, and, as always, her bed sheets were soaked in sweat.

She looked down at her hands, no longer covered in blood, nor holding the blade she had so sought after in her dream, and they felt decidedly empty.

She may have awoken, but she certainly was not satisfied.

Her jolt had robbed her of her kill, snapping her back to consciousness, and having been deprived of it when she had been so desperately close, only made her want it all the more.

She growled a deep, threatening and animalistic sound in the back of her throat, though she had no idea why, and in the cold darkness of the early morning, the great longing and the unquenchable lust for blood, for stone cold murder, overwhelmed the still young Vivian Featherstone, taunting and tormenting her in its entirety.

After another week, Vivian's trial seemed to be going well, and the House that she had set up was working most efficiently. Though it had taken a little time, she was now finding that fewer and fewer issues were filtering through to her, and they were only ever the most serious or complicated problems.

She had spent quite some time explaining to her volunteers exactly how she had wanted things to be dealt with, and that if the system proved to be successful, she would reward them with full time, paid employment, a concept so far unheard of for the running of Virtus.

She had thought it a nice incentive, and entrusted Archer with the maintenance of the House's pay, and his own, now that his other duties had been greatly reduced.

He seemed, thankfully, to be much more relaxed about the whole situation, and even relatively satisfied at its success, though he couldn't help but slip in comments now and then that it should have been set up months ago.

Regardless though, the volume of his responsibilities had most definitely been eased, and so he was much more content in his day-to-day work, now able to give more time to those issues that most required his attention.

Considering all that, and that she had promised to go to Jared's aid in the south, Vivian decided to put her new system to the test.

After telling Archer that she was going to leave for the southern farms, and being pleasantly surprised that he barely even batted an eyelid, Vivian set out with renewed vigour, knowing that, with any luck, she wouldn't come back to a mountain of issues.

But, as she had explained to them, they needed to learn to cope without her, for the time would one day come of course when she wouldn't be there for them to fall back on.

Why she had been so specific when she had told them that, she didn't really know. The words just seemed to flow off her tongue automatically, and her new collection of advisors had seemed to simply take them as gospel.

And so, just like that, it was settled.

Passing her responsibility over to them, Vivian left her house in the centre of the city and, certainly not for the first time, headed south. Though this time she moved with clear purpose and definite intent.

8

As ever, travelling through Virtus brought with it the usual issues, but, somewhat gladly, Vivian redirected those to her newly appointed House, ensuring her people that she was on an errand of great importance, and that their queries would still be dealt with in the same way.

Of course some people grumbled that she was not going to help them personally, and immediately, but then they would simply have to get used to that. She had always known this day would eventually come, one way or another.

In fact, it felt good to pass on some of her responsibility, for she had not had a break from it even once since she had returned here, save her occasional side trip out to Featherstone Keep.

The journey south wasn't really a long one, even though the farm she sought was on the furthest southern reaches of town. She had set out late however, and it had already been past noon when she'd left, meaning she would have to stay one night in a hostel or an inn of some sort, before reaching Jared's farm the next day.

To be perfectly honest though, Vivian enjoyed such trips, for it gave her a much better chance to see exactly how her people were really faring.

"Vivian!" The owner greeted her as she approached the inn an hour or two later. She had stayed there once before and, naturally, he remembered her - few ever forgot her.

"Good evening Nicholas." She replied, smiling warmly and taking his hand.

"Here for the night again?" He asked, as always jumping straight to business. Perhaps that was the reason she liked him so.

"Please." She responded, nodding her head.

"Of course!" He beamed. "But of course. No charge." He added with a wink. "Not for our saviour!"

"You're too kind." Vivian thanked him, a little dryly admittedly, but he seemed not to notice.

"If you need anything just ask." He assured her, handing Vivian the keys to her room for the night.

"Thank you." She repeated, taking the key from his outstretched hand and smiling gratefully. "I will."

Barely minutes later Vivian climbed the single flight of stairs, passed by the flaking paintwork along the narrow corridors, and reached her assigned room. The door eventually opened after she had worked the key in the latch for a few minutes, and she closed it gently behind her as she entered.

There was a small single bed in the middle of the room, a creaky looking chest of drawers, a full length mirror on the one free wall, surrounded by peeling paint, and a moderately dirty washroom.

If she was perfectly honest, the room was in little better condition than the rest of the inn, but then, it didn't really matter, she was only there to sleep.

However, though it was her sole purpose of being there, sleep did not come easily to Vivian that night, and when it did, it came in fitful and restless bursts.

Her dreams, when and where she was able to catch them, were plagued again by terrible nightmares. It was nothing new, and she had come to live with them over the years, but recently they seemed to have been getting more and more out of hand.

She found herself running from something, fleeing blindly through trees and forests and streets and alleys, being chased and pursued by a great shadow that loomed over her immensely. And the shadow of whatever monster it was shrieked and screeched in great echoing cries that resonated all around her.

Mercifully, unlike some dreams of the past, this one did not really last all that long, and within minutes of running, Vivian awoke with another jolt, gasping for breath, desperately pulling oxygen into her burning lungs. Her body shook and she stood stooped over with her hands on her knees, her legs throbbing and heavy.

Why did her legs hurt so much?

Looking up and glancing around, her eyes adjusting to the darkness, Vivian found herself stood in a narrow alleyway, the sky dark far above her, and silence all around.

She had actually been running, she realised, both in her dream, and in reality. How in the world she'd managed to do that, she had no idea, but now that her breath was returning to her, Vivian immediately began to think about getting back to the inn, trying not to panic.

Clearly her nightmares were getting worse, but at that moment it didn't matter to her how she'd got there, now she just needed to get back. She was dressed in nothing but her underclothes, obviously not having stopped to think about getting dressed in her sleep, and she was, unsurprisingly, freezing.

But then, before she could turn to retrace her steps the way she'd come, a great dread and emptiness washed over her, and her hand reached automatically for the blade at her waist. Though, of course, it was not there. She never carried one in fact, yet her fingers always seemed to yearn for it. The longing desire for bloodlust filled her once more, and she gritted her teeth resolutely.

She would just have to wait for it to pass: ride it out.

But, on this occasion, that simply wasn't to be.

Strong hands grabbed her from behind then, the man's arms wrapping around her comparatively small body easily, encompassing her in the darkness. Vivian tried to scream for help, opening her mouth and drawing a deep breath to shriek, but his arm clamped immovably about her neck, crushing her windpipe, and he forced his hand roughly over her mouth, making it impossible for her to call for aid.

He pulled out a blade then and pressed it harshly to her cheek, its face cold and threatening against hers.

Crime was low in Virtus, Vivian had made sure of that. But, as is the nature of the sorrowful human condition, regardless of the location, such a thing is ever-present.

"You're very pretty." The man's disgusting voice whispered in her ear, his words dripping with an indescribable hunger, but then, Vivian too had a lust and a hunger all of her own.

She tried to struggle and worm away from his grasp, but she failed with each attempt, and with every effort she made, the man grew in confidence, knowing he had her.

"Now…" He whispered slowly and intently. "You're not going to scream, because if you do, I'm going to cut your face into chunks…"

His threat might have been an empty one, but Vivian somehow doubted it, as he pressed the blade harder against her face, drawing some blood as he did so. She felt the warm liquid streak down her cheek and drip onto her exposed front.

Either way, whether he was bluffing or not, she did as he instructed, and stayed perfectly quiet and still.

He threw her to the ground then, manhandling her without a care. But, painful as it was, Vivian made not a peep.

Within an instant he was on her, blade no longer in hand, for by now he felt totally in control, and he loved it. Instead, his hands grabbed and raked hungrily at Vivian's body and underclothes, desperately trying to rip them from her exposed skin to get to her, driven by his own desire for dominance.

It wasn't long before he succeeded, smashing Vivian's head against the cold stone floor in the process, knocking the sense from her for a moment, allowing him the perfect opportunity to strip her naked. He seized his chance and ripped what remained of her clothes from her body, revealing all that lay beneath.

He took a moment to admire Vivian flawless figure in the darkness, though battered and bruised from the assault he had delivered it may have been.

The slight jingling of his belt then snapped Vivian back to her senses, but before she could react, he was upon her again, pressing his body down of top of hers, pinning her back to the freezing ground with his own weight.

He chuckled a low, throaty and disgusting laugh as he did so. It was the sound of terrible victory, though he hadn't quite yet claimed his prize.

Unbeknownst to him though, he had unwittingly chosen Vivian Featherstone to prey on with his sick desires, and in the darkness of the alleyway, Vivian had materialised a blade of her own from thin air. Concealing it carefully beneath her hand so that its shine did not alert her attacker to its existence, she held firm, and waited for her own chance to strike.

She could quite easily have stopped him a number of different ways, and in fact much earlier. She had never needed to let it go this far, for now she was totally exposed and vulnerable, and he pressed heavily down on top of her, pushing himself as close to her as he could.

But this felt more real, and Vivian's lust for bloody revenge was far too great to let this opportunity pass by unseized.

Quite simply, nothing else would have sufficed.

He grabbed her thighs roughly and forced her across the stones painfully, scratching and scraping her back, drawing yet more blood. This was it. He was about to claim his prize. But it was far too late however, and there was absolutely nothing he could do.

By the time he finally realised who she was, and what she was about to do, he was powerless to stop it.

Catching a flash of Vivian's shining blue eyes in the darkness, just before he descended upon her, fear caught in the predator's throat.

He opened his mouth to speak, to cry, to shout, to do anything, but instead of words coming tumbling out, instead came great flurries and torrents of blood, as Vivian's concealed blade slashed viciously across his unprotected neck.

Great floods of blood poured from his gaping throat then, covering Vivian completely, showering her in his torturous death, and she revelled in it. His body began to convulse and jerk terribly, and she jumped up and launched herself at him, stabbing and slashing wildly with barely any direction at all, screaming like an absolute lunatic as she did so, completely lost to herself and to her awful desires.

Barely a minute later, those sixty seconds having flashed by in a heartbeat, Vivian stood over the man, no longer predator, but instead prey, her victory complete, and adrenaline coursed through her veins like wildfire.

Her breathing was heavy and she felt sticky, like she had done in her dream, though now her whole naked body was saturated in blood, and her devolution had taken a second, enormous step.

Vivian revelled in the glory of her success for a while, remaining standing naked and streaked in blood over the now lifeless body of her attacker.

Waist deep in that magnificent, vengeful feeling - nothing could have been better.

But then the terrible emptiness and the dreadful longing washed over her once again, as her coursing adrenaline faded and dwindled. She dropped to her knees, knocking them heavily into the cold, harsh stone.

Feeling yet again incomplete and unfulfilled, Vivian sobbed and screamed in the dark of the night, horrified at her own actions.

Yet, even still, though now it was over, and the wonderful feeling had come and gone, passing by in barely an instant, she wanted nothing more than to do it all over again.

9

Luckily the morning was still dark, and the streets desolate, allowing Vivian to race back through the ice cold alleyways without being seen. Her underclothes having been ripped to shreds by her attacker, she sprinted naked along the streets, covered from head to toe in slowly drying and flaking blood.

Her feet ached from running barefoot on stone and cobble, but as much as they hurt, even catching a few times and bleeding fresh, she did not stop. She couldn't risk it. She absolutely had to get back without being seen, and the first rays of sunlight were already peeking their way over the far eastern horizon.

Thankfully, mercy seemingly on her side, Vivian crept back into the inn, managing to climb up the uneven stonework and sidle in through her room's single open window.

Perhaps she had crept out this way in the night?

In her sleep…?

She had no idea, and at that point it really didn't matter. All that mattered was that she'd made it back without being seen, she hoped. Kael had proved to her of late however that she wasn't always as inconspicuous as she'd thought, or perhaps it was simply that he was just very observant and keen eyed.

Vivian stopped for a moment, ceasing all movement, her mind wandering.

Kael.

Suddenly, from her spreading thoughts, Vivian felt a huge wave of guilt that filled her with a dreadful sense of completion.

He could never know.

He would be ashamed of her.

Everybody would.

Pushing the thoughts from her mind, trying desperately to focus, Vivian proceeded immediately to scrub every inch of her body, splashing and soaking herself with water from a bowl in the washroom. The bowl had been stood there all night, and she shivered and gritted her teeth as the ice cold liquid ran down her face and front.

It took a long time to wash her entire body clean, removing all evidence and disposing of the water so that no one would ever know. By that time the sun had already risen, and the scurrying noise of people outside and in the rooms next door to hers could be heard.

She breathed a heavy sigh of relief, reluctantly running over that night's events in her mind. Clearly her nightmares were getting worse.

But why?

How?

She had no idea.

Turning then and glancing in the full length mirror on the wall, Vivian looked her naked body up and down, sighing as she did so.

Obviously she was young, and without a shadow of a doubt would have been very attractive to any young man, for her body had grown and formed in a very womanly way, and it was most pleasing to the eye.

Her gaze however, did not see those things, but instead came to rest upon the scars that marked her body, forming and capturing both the worst and best memories of her life.

The silvery scar on her chest, angled between her ribs, was from when she had faced the Greystones upon her return to Virtus. She remembered with a chill the feel of the sword sliding and grating between her ribcage.

She had removed it, she recalled the events of that day, casting her eyes down to her hands now, and her palms were still scarred from dragging the great blade from within her. Those ones were faded and barely even visible, but she could still just about make them out.

And then of course there were the burns on her back. She turned, looking over her shoulder, and examined her back in the mirror, seeing the mottled skin warped and gruesome looking in a perfectly rounded circle on her upper back, directly between her shoulder blades.

That, of course, was from when she had attempted to go to Red's aid during their final battle together, just before he had been killed...

Vivian looked over all her scars, sorrowfully at first, but then also with a smile, the glimmer of contented memories coming to her mind.

She had healed those grave wounds before killing the Grey, leaving only these comparatively small scars, and Vivian was certain she could have even healed those completely too. It would have been a simple thing to do, to return her skin to its original, flawless complexion, but even so, she never had done.

She simply couldn't.

They reminded her too much of Red.

The morning air was fresh and clear and it filled Vivian's lungs with its cool, revitalising hands. Above the great city the clouds drifted by lazily, relaxed and calm, not too great in number, wandering now and then in front of the sun and blocking its rays, but never for more than a minute or two.

After recovering her composure and redressing, Vivian bade the innkeeper farewell, and headed southwards once more. She pushed the incidents of that night from her thoughts as best she could, forgetting them, at least for now, and wondered what in the world was happening to her.

Vivian thought then of Red, and what in the world he would think if he knew what had become of her. It didn't matter. There was nothing she could do about it. She just had to keep going, and nobody could ever know, especially Kael.

Bizarrely then, as she thought of the stranger from the north that she had pursued through the Redwoods, she felt oddly guilty, for her thoughts of him had interrupted her thoughts of Red.

She knew of course that her guilt was ridiculous, for such a thing was not a crime, but nonetheless, she couldn't help but feel as though things were changing.

Yes, it seemed that change was definitely upon her.

And people do so fear change, often for good reason, though it is never without purpose.

The people greeted her pleasantly as she headed towards Jared's farm, occasionally approaching her to ask how she was, and Vivian enquired about their lives in turn. That was something she always tried her utmost to do: to show an interest in each and every one of those she cared and looked out for. Though, naturally, she knew that was impossible. There were simply too many people for her to know so much about all of them, but still she tried her hardest.

Jared too, unsurprisingly, was delighted to see Vivian enter the front gates of his humble farmstead, and the wearied look about his eyes told Vivian all that she needed to know.

Clearly the attacks had not ceased.

"Miss Featherstone!" He greeted Vivian, walking towards her with his arms outstretched welcomingly. "It's such a pleasure to finally meet you!" He continued.

"Likewise." Vivian replied with a smile and a nod of her head. "How are you faring?" She asked then, quite seriously, glancing around briefly at the farmstead.

From what she could see everything looked, for the most part, very normal. There was, however, an unmistakeable look about the faces of all who lived and worked there. A deep, underlying fear of the unknown plagued them all, and though their spirits soared at the sight of their saviour, even that was not enough to suppress the terror that gripped them.

"Not too well…" Jared replied honestly, sighing deeply and allowing his shoulders to slump slightly.

He too glanced around then. He saw the small thatched homes of his people, the mills and storage barns dotted here and there, seemingly without order, but with an organisation that suited the needs of his farmstead ideally. And then too his eyes fell to the barn in the distance, set back a little ways from everything else, and much closer to the tree line of the Redwoods, only just beyond it.

Around the barn grazed cattle, though with every other step each of them looked up and surveyed the forest edge nervously, as if waiting for the inevitable.

"There haven't been attacks every night." Jared continued to explain. "But on the nights that there have…" He shuddered at the thought, as if there was no need for further explanation.

"Ok." Vivian concluded, gathering that this wasn't the sort of thing he wished to discuss so publically. "I hope the messenger I sent arrived in good time?" She asked Jared then.

She knew of course that her message had been received, for Jared had sent one in return to her abode, but for some reason, a reason that eluded her even as she spoke her words, Vivian felt the need to ask.

"Yes, thank you." He replied pleasantly. "I received them both. I was very glad to hear from you if I'm honest."

Vivian started for a moment, confusion crossing her face.

"Both?" Vivian questioned. "What do you mean, both?"

"The elderly gentleman you sent…" Jared explained first, a little confused. "He came saying he had spoken with you, purely by chance, and had offered to carry your message here himself. He told me that you were coming to our aid…"

"Yes, that's right." Vivian confirmed. "What of the second?"

"The younger gentleman." Jared began. "Nice fellow, strange name though, I can't quite remember it now; he told me that he was here to help my watchmen, and that when you came along he would be helping you search for the monster, or whatever it is that's doing this…"

His voice dropped low with that sentence; though of course it was no secret, it was not the sort of thing Jared enjoyed making public conversation about.

"I think he works for my cousin, Linton…" Jared continued. "On the west side of the city…"

"Kael!?" Vivian exclaimed, shocked and surprised and pleased all at once, her heart racing and jumping into her mouth with excitement at the thought that he was here.

"That's his name!" Jared replied, gesturing expansively with his hands.

And then, before either of them could say another word, a voice sounded beside them, approaching from the direction of the barn in the distance, his approach up until that point inconspicuous and unnoticed, as it always was.

Vivian turned as Kael spoke, the sound of his voice music to her ears, lifting her spirits enormously.

She forgot the darkness of the recent past almost instantly, and her renewed blue eyes came to rest on his face adoringly.

"Hello stranger."

10

Perhaps there was only one word to describe how Vivian felt at that moment. She was entirely, completely and utterly, speechless. Her mouth opened and closed and then opened again uselessly, unable to make even the hint of a sound.

The tugging pain in her heart, the one that had taken up residence there ever since Kael's absence, now subsided, and she felt almost wholly recovered, somehow fulfilled, and she could see by the look on his face and the adoration in his eyes that he felt the same way.

Jared didn't quite know what was happening, but as he stood there for a moment, awed by the connection so clear between the great Vivian Featherstone and this stranger, Kael, he couldn't help but smile, for he was old enough to know the beginnings of love when he saw it.

Eventually, after a few minutes, still neither of them having spoken, Jared coughed lightly, bringing his hand up to his mouth in a fist, breaking the silence, filled so fully with everything except words.

"Kael…" Vivian eventually managed, stirred by Jared's action, glancing between the two of them.

Amidst all the trouble and anguish that Jared had surely been undergoing, he threw Vivian a knowing smile, and politely excused himself.

"I'm afraid I have matters to attend to…" He lied pleasantly. "Kael, you've been here a good few days now, do you think you could show Miss

Featherstone around the farmstead and explain to her exactly what's been happening. I'm sure you've heard all the stories by now…"

"Of course sir." Kael replied casually. "It would be my pleasure."

Vivian remained dumbfounded.

"Excellent." Jared concluded then, clapping his hands together. "I shall meet you both over by the barn an hour before sundown." He told them, before bidding them both a good day and turning immediately on his heel, leaving the two of them standing alone.

Silence ensued again then for a few more moments before Vivian eventually found her tongue.

"What are you doing here?" She asked Kael, still unable to take her eyes from him. Of course Jared had already told her why Kael had come, but then, that hadn't been the real reason.

"I had to see you again." He replied immediately, without even a trace of embarrassment in his voice with his admission. "This was my only chance."

"You volunteered to watch the cattle?" Vivian questioned, and Kael nodded in response. "But you've been here almost a week!" She exclaimed then, for some reason upset by the fact, and, perhaps more so, by his reckless foolishness. "You know what's been happening!!" She pressed. "You could have been killed!!"

"I wasn't though." He replied calmly. "There haven't been any attacks since I arrived."

"You didn't know there wouldn't be any attacks!" Vivian snapped back then, her heart fluttering with worry at the thought that he might have been harmed.

Kael only shrugged.

"Must be fate then." He concluded simply, somehow calming all of Vivian's worries in an instant. "It worked, you're here, and I'm still alive."

Again, Vivian was thunderstruck, with absolutely no idea how to respond. That word fate rang true with her, and Red's face flashed momentarily before her eyes, and in that fleeting glance, the great red bear's expression bore the resemblances of content upon in, pleased with what he saw.

Saying not another word, not even sure that she could, Vivian raced forward and caught Kael up in a crushing embrace. He squeezed her back and held her tightly, knowing now that he'd done the right thing by risking his life here, without a shadow of a doubt.

"No one has heard them during the day yet." Kael explained to Vivian as they walked, exploring and examining the boundaries of Jared's farmstead. "But it's true what everyone's been saying about the howls at night. Even though there haven't been any attacks, I've heard them myself. There are many different ones, but they all come together, and sometimes there's even a great roaring and shrieking too. The howls are probably wolves..." Kael reasoned. But I have absolutely no idea what else it could be..."

"Are they as bad as people have been saying?" Vivian asked.

"Probably worse." Kael admitted. "They're coming from a long way off south, towards the mountains, that much I can tell. But it sounds as though they're right there." He explained, emphasising his point by simply holding his hand out a foot from his face.

They reached the barn then, as they had been following the line of red trunks round in a vast arc. Even from a distance Vivian had been able to see the damage the building had suffered, and great chunks were missing from its sides, and the doors were practically hanging off their hinges.

What little of the barn that was still left intact, barely keeping the flimsy structure standing, was smeared with thick lashes of blood and other substances, most of which Vivian didn't wish to even try to name.

"Oh dear." Vivian commented, in something of a drastic understatement, coming to a halt before the pitiful looking assembly of broken planks and shattered walls.

"Hmm…" Kael replied, admitting with that simple sound that he had indeed been terrified the past few nights, waiting eagerly for Vivian's arrival.

They continued on and Kael showed Vivian the farmstead in its entirety. It was a humble and clearly hard earned establishment, and the people toiled away in the fields, forever glancing nervously over their shoulders, all too aware of the seemingly great danger they were in.

"So that's pretty much it." Kael eventually concluded, as they once again reached the main gate of the farm, the sun dipping quite low in the sky by now. Vivian looked up and over to the horizon to their west, over the tops of the vast sea of Redwoods.

"It's almost an hour until sunset. Let's go and meet Jared." She decided, and Kael nodded in agreement, leading the way back off towards the barn.

Only ten minutes later they reached their destination, arriving at virtually the same time as Jared and two other men, much bigger and burlier than the rest Vivian had seen here.

"Ah! Excellent!" Jared the farmstead owner exclaimed as he approached Vivian and Kael. "My friends, please may I introduce you to Heath, and Kandor." He introduced the two men in his company, gesturing to each of them in turn. "Gentlemen." He continued, looking to the two muscular men then. "This is Miss Vivian Featherstone, and her splendid and generous companion, Kael."

"Pleasure." Heath greeted them in a deep, gruff voice, shaking each of their hands in turn, dwarfing them with his massive hands like shovels. Kandor did the same and nodded in acknowledgement, smiling at Vivian and Kael with crooked teeth but kind eyes.

They both wore thick hides that covered their massive shoulders and torsos, and each looked to be padded with tough leather. Strapped to their waists were large swords that looked too heavy to lift, though Vivian imagined the two men before her wielded them as easily as she would have a feather.

Their hair was cut short, almost to stubble, and they both wore the makings of beards, though they were cropped at least weekly. Clearly they had both spent much of their lives outdoors, and their skin was worn like rough leather.

"Heath and Kandor have kindly volunteered to assist you on the night watches." Jared explained. "I've heard they have some experience in this field…" He added evasively, looking over the enormous bulks of his two hired guards. "I can imagine they make rather formidable allies." He finished, smiling with hope that was at least half false.

"Excellent. Thank you." Vivian said, smiling at the two men in turn. "We'll be leaving the cattle in the fields." She told Jared then.

"Is that wise?" Jared asked, concerned slightly. "The fields stretch far alongside the trees. It will make the cattle much harder to watch."

"They won't be straying close to the trees." Vivian explained patiently. "They're too afraid. And the Redwoods will tell me if anything is approaching."

Jared nodded in mutual agreement then, his eyes going slightly wide, but, knowing that Vivian's power was likely not simple fable, he didn't question it.

"Very well." He finally concluded. "If there's anything else you need, please don't hesitate to ask."

"Torches, please." Kael requested immediately. "We need to mount torches on poles."

"Mounted torches?" Jared questioned.

"Yes. So that we can see too." Kael replied, casting a quick smile to Vivian, and she was forced to look away save blushing. "We'll need to light the field."

99

"Very well." Jared accepted, looking up to the rapidly darkening sky. "I shall arrange it immediately."

"Thank you." Vivian said finally, nodding her head. "We'll stop this Jared." Vivian assured the nervous farmstead owner, smiling as reassuringly as possible.

"I hope so." Jared agreed. "If anyone can, it's you…"

Within the hour Kael had received his flaming torches as requested, each one tied to the end of a broomstick pole, which he immediately placed at regular intervals along the treeline. The four of them then set up in the barn, overlooking the fields through the broken panels in the walls, and prepared to settle in for the night.

The idea of Kael's torches was to illuminate their entire perimeter, hopefully spotlighting any approaching threat for those without Vivian's supreme senses, whilst, at the same time, not giving away their position. The last thing they wanted to do was highlight their position, and leave the area they were supposed to be watching dark.

And so, as the night set in, and darkness fell over the farmstead and the fields surrounding it, the farmhands all retreated to the relative safety of their homes, bolting their doors and barricading their windows.

Vivian and Kael and their two companions settled down also, but instead of in a secure, locked building, then nestled as comfortably as they could in the cold, draughty and exposed barn.

The Redwoods Rise and Fall

The sun disappeared along with all remnants of its warmth, vanishing mysteriously over the horizon, replaced by a perfectly clear sky, illuminated by the cold light of the moon and a thousand stars dotted across the rich, dark blue blanket above.

Wearing heavily on, the night passed by slowly and with watchful eyes set upon the trees. All night long, as the eerie silence and the endless darkness laid over them, Vivian and Kael sat close, side by side, almost touching, but not quite, barely daring to even breathe.

As time passed however, their torches flickered in the distance, stretching off in both directions, and the cattle grazed and slept and flitted here and there, moving very nervously. The Redwoods covering the distance to the south swayed and frothed and bellowed like a great, seething ocean in the breeze, fluid and tranquil, but at the same time immovable.

But there were no roars or howls to be heard, and nothing disturbed their defensive line of flames, and, though nervous beyond measure, the cattle remained untouched.

Morning eventually raised its head, and though they were wearied from their night of watchfulness, the four of them emerged from the barn unscathed.

Their uneventful night had left them all wondering whether their presence had deterred the attacker, or attackers, and whether it or they had known they were lying in wait. Nonetheless though, they were not discouraged, knowing that there had been a run of nights of late where no attacks had taken place, and they simply set up again the following night.

Settling down again in waiting, Vivian and Kael sat a little closer together, comforted by each other's warmth, but yet again, the night passed without incident.

Four days and four nights passed in a similar fashion, with not a hint of sound or a flicker of movement to be heard or seen. And with each night and day that passed, though she was more and more wearied, Vivian was only all the more determined to not give up.

In the end, somehow knowing that their efforts here were futile, and clearly fruitless, Vivian came to a decision.

It was on the morning of the fifth day, when Jared approached them cautiously and inquisitively, as he had done every morning, seeking news of the night's events, that Vivian informed him of her decision.

"Nothing again?" He asked, his voice peaking. He had been undecided over the past week or so whether the lack of attacks was a good thing, or simply the quiet before the storm…

"Jared…" Vivian began, rubbing her heavy eyes with the base of her palms. It had been another long, uneventful night, and her body felt sluggish. "I think it's me." She began to explain.

"You?" Jared asked, confused. "How can it be you?"

"I think that this creature, or these creatures, whatever it is, can sense my presence. I'm not exactly the most inconspicuous soul around…"

"Right…" Jared replied, admittedly still confused. "What are you trying to say? You're not leaving are you?" The concern in his voice was evident.

Vivian had already spoken to her three watch companions, who had all eagerly agreed to her proposal, as by now they were beginning to get rather frustrated by the whole ordeal, or perhaps, more accurately, the lack of one.

"We're going to head south, into the Redwoods, and find whatever this thing is." Vivian stated, her tone very matter of fact.

"I see…" Jared started. "But what if you leave and it comes back?"

His question was an obvious one, and indeed Vivian had thought the matter over repeatedly, considering every such detail.

"If it tries to go around us, the Redwoods will warn me, and I shall return."

Jared nodded then in response, though again his eyes widened slightly at the thought. He just took her word as gospel and left it at that.

"Very well then." He concluded, clasping his hands together and adjusting his dirtied over shirt. "When do you leave?"

Vivian Featherstone looked up at the morning sky, slightly more clouded than the past few days, and bit her lip for a moment, thinking.

Finally, she looked back to Jared.

"Immediately." She replied, her voice steady and levelled. "We leave now."

11

It had taken them perhaps two or three hours to gather supplies and equipment, carrying only the bare essentials that they needed. Kael was experienced enough with travel through the vast forest anyway, they were home to Vivian, obviously, and Heath and Kandor did not seem in the least bit phased by the notion. As a matter of fact, they seemed quite invigorated by the whole idea.

Soon enough they were trekking through the undergrowth and between the seas of vast trunks, moving at a steady pace in a single file.

Vivian moved with the precision and confidence of someone who was perfectly at home. Kael's movements were similarly expert, though he was clearly slightly more cautious and nervous than Vivian. And Heath and Kandor, though obviously unafraid, crashed through the bush in a manner that made Vivian visibly cringe, for the whisperings in her ears asked continually of her why they were so careless.

It wasn't that they were overly thoughtless though, Vivian over time realised; it was simply that their powerful, muscular bulks were so tall and so wide that it simply was not possibly for them to apply stealth to the same extent as Vivian and Kael did. And so, she did not hold their conspicuousness against them, and simply gave them pointers here and there, helping them to quieten their rampaging steps, even if only slightly.

They travelled in the direction of the vast mountain ranges, heading generally in a south to south westerly direction, cutting through the Redwoods with ease as Vivian led them onwards.

Several days passed, but yet still they found nothing. Aside from general wildlife and game, the forest was desolate of anything even remotely resembling a predator, and the Redwoods were quiet on the matter themselves, giving Vivian not even the hint of a clue.

Overnight they slept in huddles round a small fire, taking turns one at a time on watch. But even those efforts seemed wasted, and they slept soundly for three nights running.

It was not to last however, and on the fourth night, unbeknownst to Kael or Heath or Kandor, Vivian did not sleep restfully at all, and she tossed and turned and jerked in fits and starts as she dreamt.

In her mind's eye, her vision blurred and hazy, Vivian saw Kael being chased endlessly through the thick woodlands. He threw terrified glances over his shoulder as he ran, charging through the trees and bushes, forcing his way through each, bashing and cutting himself painfully as he did so.

What exactly he was being chased by, Vivian didn't know. All she could see from where she stood between the trees was a great looming shadow hulking its way after him, somehow melting through the trees without effort, as if it belonged there.

Was it the same shadow that had chased her through the streets, barely a week ago?

Every time she tried to run to Kael's aid, or shout for help, she was stopped, restrained by some invisible force, unable to move or even speak.

She could only watch on helplessly as he was tracked and hunted and pursued, until finally, at the last moment, when the shadowy beast was finally upon him, Vivian startled awake.

The piercing shriek that she released then when she awoke must have carried for a goodly way in every direction, for it practically shook the ground as she let it fly.

"KAEL!!!" She screamed, bolting upright and startling her companions immediately awake also.

"Vivian!!" Kael responded instantly, darting to her side. "What is it!?" What's wrong!?"

Burying her head in her hands, her shoulders shaking violently, Vivian tried to calm her racing breaths, and her heart pounded heavily in her chest like a thunderous drumbeat.

Kael rested his arms gently round Vivian's shoulders, feeling her body shaking with every movement, and Heath and Kandor looked on helplessly, just as she had done in her dream, unable to help and not knowing what to do.

Suddenly then, as they glanced up for a moment, Kael and Heath and Kandor all felt their breath catch in their throats, and their bodies tensed rigidly, fear and uncertainty gripping them.

None of them dared move. Kael's hand still rested on Vivian's back, but even by that simple touch she still felt his body tense, and she looked up between her heavy breaths. But when she did, her breaths too stopped, and she rose slowly to her feet, her eyes flitting all around.

Encircling them in the trees, just as had happened to her and Kael when they had first met by Featherstone Keep, they were surrounded by a flurry of woodland animals. This time however, though their expressions were identically expectant and longing, there were hundreds upon thousands of them, packed in so tightly next to each other that wolves brushed coats with deer and hogs and bears, uncaringly, for their attention was focused so intently upon Vivian.

What were they doing?

At first glance, nothing, it seemed. Just watching, and listening, their eyes resting heavily upon the young, burdened Featherstone, afraid and imploring.

Something stirred then and caught Vivian's attention. She whipped her head around, her senses edgy and tight. But when none of her three companions moved, she realised all of a sudden that the sounds were in her mind only.

Closing her eyes carefully, Vivian opened her mind to the Redwoods, pleased to feel them reaching out to her, for the first time in a very long time.

When they spoke, their hundreds upon thousands of voices rang clearly in her thoughts, their words embedded with generations upon generations of knowledge and truth. More powerful and resonant than ever before, their voices sounded certain and endless.

"Vivian." They implored, speaking for every animal that they encompassed. "Vivian, they need you once more…"

The words struck a shiver down Vivian's spine, chilling her to the bone.

But before she could begin to reply, or even think about what the Redwoods meant, her concentration was interrupted, shattered by a great bellowing shriek that echoed and raced through the trees terribly and hungrily.

There came the unsettling howls and bays that had been described to her so many times, and they reached Vivian's ears yearningly, as if they had sought after her for years. And then, following immediately, came a sound that terrified Vivian beyond measure, for she had never heard anything of such immensity, not even during all her years spent with Red and Clover.

The roar that shook the trees then, and even the very ground itself, crashed into them with such devastating terror that the creatures all around them scattered immediately, fleeing for their lives in every direction, simply at the sound of it.

It reminded Vivian of the tale her father used to tell her as a girl: the one about the dragon, who when it roared it could be heard for hundreds of leagues in every direction. She had forever told herself that such a creature could never exist. But the bellow that echoed around them still, shaking the very ground beneath their feet, told her otherwise.

She shook off the notion resolutely however, trying to clear her head, along with the ringing in her ears.

Within seconds, the four of them were stood alone once more, her three companion's faces a picture, their mouths agape, and the blood drained from their faces.

They were only stories, they were only stories, Vivian kept telling herself, repeating it over and over again, forcing herself to believe it, though fear gripped her heart fiercely. They were fairy tales of knights and heroes and monsters.

The blood of the forests and of the animals may have changed, but dragons didn't exist, they couldn't.

It was impossible.

12

Continuing south relentlessly, Vivian led her three companions on through the Redwoods, still heading towards the howls and the roars in the direction on the mountains, growing ever louder by the hour. They were all much more wary now, though they had by no means been careless to begin with, and they all jumped at the slightest sound. Even Vivian, with her vast experience in the woodlands, and her extraordinary senses and power, felt blind and helpless, as if something was blocking what she so desperately needed to see.

Something was definitely wrong. She didn't need her powers to see that. She could sense it. She could feel it, right through to her very bones.

After another hour the cold morning light was creeping through the canopy above them, and Vivian looked up as the early rays streamed across her face, warm and comforting against her cool skin.

"What is it?" Kael asked, keeping his voice low so that only Vivian could hear.

"Nothing." Vivian lied automatically, and very unconvincingly. She had learned over the years to hide her true feelings from those around her, so as not to attract unnecessary attention and questions.

For some reason though, regardless of the fact she'd changed nothing about her guise, Kael saw straight through her façade.

"Okay." Kael replied. "But what's wrong?" He asked, smirking slightly.

Vivian sighed, having known she wouldn't have been able to convince him, she decided instead just to open up.

"I don't know what's going on." She admitted. "I don't know what this thing is, and I can't sense it…"

"Neither can we." Kael assured her, but Vivian shook her head.

"I know." She replied, exasperated. "But I'm supposed to have all this power!" She hissed, clenching her teeth, desperately trying to keep her voice low. "I can't even sense a few bloody wolves."

"How do you know its wolves?" Kael asked then.

"What other animals do you know that howls?" She questioned.

"Fair enough…" Kael admitted. "But I know a lot of animals that roar, and none of them roar like that…"

For that remark, Vivian had no answer, for indeed he was right. The only thing she'd ever heard that had come anywhere close to such a sound had been Red's terrifying bellows, and yet even they had paled in comparison.

Then, as if on cue, a chorus of baying howls and bellowing roars ripped through the trees, closer than ever before.

Vivian and Kael darted from each other's sides, and Heath and Kandor did the same, each of them sprinting desperately for cover. Vivian merged herself with a massively thick trunk to her left, pressing her back against it for all she was worth.

Heath crouched low in the thickest shrubs he could find, and Kandor did the same, just to his right.

Kael had the same idea, but, unfortunately, fate had not favoured him in that moment.

As he bounded round the back of a tree, eyes fixed on a small, dense shrub that would easily have concealed him, he failed to notice the small, grey pressure plate protruding up barely an inch from the ground, half covered by fallen leaves and loose moss.

There was but the tiniest of clicks as Kael's foot pressed the plate down, his bodyweight releasing the sprung mechanism all too easily.

Vivian saw it just too late, and in the blink of an eye, far too short a time for her to call out a warning, the monstrous metal jaws ripped from beneath their light covering of earth, and snapped fiercely shut.

Of course though, this time, the jaws were not empty when they closed, moving with such frightening speed and force, and instead Kael's leg was between them.

The result was dreadful.

Without even the slightest hint of a fight, for it stood no chance, Kael's leg shattered in the trap, as the teeth destroyed the muscles and tendons and ligaments about his knee, butchering them with ease. As for the joint itself, it collapsed in terribly, crunching horribly as it did so, having had no defence against such a thing.

Kael crumpled to the floor, overcome in an instant by the blinding pain of his leg being destroyed, and screeched in agony. Writhing about on the floor, his senses were paralysed by the anguish of his injury. He desperately tried to free his leg from the trap, but even if he could have done, it would have yielded nothing.

Vivian screamed and rushed over to him, her heart leaping immediately into her mouth, knocking aside her senses too.

"KAEL!!" She shrieked, charging forward and throwing herself at his side, staring disbelievingly at his ruined leg, her mouth slightly agape.

The teeth of the trap were practically touching. There was nothing left of the muscle, or anything else for that matter, that had once been round the knee. The joint itself had been destroyed entirely, held in place only by a few fragments of shattered bone, trapped between the awful manmade teeth.

He screamed again, twisting and turning desperately on the ground, but he could not escape the dreadful pain.

Then, from very close now, barely a hundred metres away, there came the terrifying sounds of snaps and growls and howls, echoing through the trees. Vivian looked to Heath and Kandor, her eyes wide and afraid, and cursed loudly and obtrusively.

"HOLD THEM BACK!" She ordered, forced to shout through both her coursing adrenaline and the need to be heard over the approaching barks and snaps.

The wolves were soon in sight, bounding hungrily through the trees.

"I HAVE TO FREE HIS LEG!"

Her two burly friends jumped immediately into action, readying their weapons: heavy swords and axes. Vivian snapped her focus back to Kael, knowing that she didn't have time to heal him, but she absolutely had to free his leg, or he would surely die.

It wasn't so much the wound she was worried about; though it was dreadful, it could be healed. Instead, it was the wolves. They had sensed Kael's distress, and has chosen that moment to strike because of it.

What in the world was going on?

Vivian pushed the thoughts from her mind and focused her will upon the trap binding what was left of Kael's leg. Though the sounds of shouting and snapping echoed in her ears, she forced the sounds away, and kept her eyes squeezed tightly shut.

For a moment she was reminded of the time long ago when she'd hidden from the shadow man in Featherstone Keep, with the sounds of fighting outside and the need to keep her eyes closed. Those thoughts too she cast from her mind however, and focused on Kael's injury.

Creaking and straining under the immense pressure, the trap slowly fought back against the powerful springs, and opened once again, freeing what was left of Kael's leg, though it's remnants hung limply from his thigh, all but destroyed completely.

He screeched again, though by now he had lost so much blood, and had so much adrenaline coursing through his veins, that he slipped in and out of consciousness from one second to the next. His head too hung limply from his shoulders, rocking from side to side, and Vivian clasped it to her chest for a moment, allowing herself a second to look around.

Immediately she wished she hadn't, as she saw exactly what had been happening all about her.

An entire pack of wolves had poured from the trees, and Heath and Kandor had met them valiantly, protecting Vivian and Kael with all their might. But the wolves descended upon them relentlessly, giving them not even a moment's respite.

The two powerful men roared and grunted and heaved and cursed as they swung their mighty weapons up and down and left and right, carving great holes in the wolves' attack. For a moment Vivian even thought they might succeed; that they would be able to fend off the attack so that they could all escape.

But it was not to be.

It was only moments later, still cradling Kael's limp head in her arms, that Vivian saw one of the wolves, apparently more intelligent and cunning than the rest, encircle the battle swiftly, moving precisely and purposefully.

"LOOK OUT!" Vivian screamed to Heath and Kandor, the desperation in her voice reaching them just as the wolf did - just a little too late.

The beast that had been encircling them darted in, keeping low to the ground, and hamstringed the both of them. Its brutal attack was both swift and efficient, sending both of Vivian's companions cascading to the ground, clutching their ruined legs, unable to stand, crying out with fresh agony.

Within seconds the swarming beasts were upon the two men, ripping at their flesh and grinding at their bones, ceasing their struggles quickly, and with very little effort, their attacks cruel and precise and without mercy.

Then, lifting their heads slowly and turning to look at Vivian, still cradling her unconscious Kael, they stalked towards her triumphantly, savouring every moment. Blood dripped from their fangs and jaws, fresh and steaming, and evil grins were spread across their furred faces.

Tears streaked down Vivian's face. But these were angry tears, for the fury within her was bubbling and boiling almost uncontrollably. She lowered Kael's head slowly to the ground, caressing him gently, and stood over him defensively, preparing herself for battle.

Levelling her gaze at the pack encircling her, Vivian saw something then that she had never expected; something that, a long time ago, she had banished from this world.

The wolves' fur was rich and jet-black, stained with blood, and their eyes, hollow and empty, were dead, and filled with the blackness of a plague so dreadful that it could mean only one thing.

It sent a chill right through to Vivian's very core, for she had seen this evil before in her lifetime, and she had committed herself to its destruction, and she had been sure that she'd succeeded.

Apparently not.

"It can't be…" Vivian whispered, her eyes wide and her heart gripped with fear.

But nonetheless, as much as she didn't want to believe it, to her senses now, clear as day, the terrible truth was apparent.

Ross Turner

Vivian drew in her will, not once taking her eyes from the wolves closing in around her, though of course she couldn't watch them all at once. Her eyes limited her, but her other senses did not, and in her mind's eye Vivian could see everything and more around her.

The first wolf attacked, lunging forward with the stealth and speed and power of an experienced killer. But nonetheless, as quick and agile as it was, Vivian was faster, and an invisible blow struck the beast mid-flight, sending it cascading heavily across a small clearing and into a thick tree trunk. Its spine snapped on impact and the beast clattered to the forest floor, twitching slightly, blood dribbling in thick spouts from its muzzle.

Vivian smiled grimly and the other wolves surrounding her bared their teeth menacingly, blood red, growling fiercely, crouching low to the ground, though hesitating slightly, ever wary of Vivian's power.

Then it began, and in a flurry of flashing teeth and fangs and crimson blood and black fur, the wolves set upon Vivian ferociously. They ripped and snapped and slashed at her, and she screamed and hammered at them in return.

The beasts were sent flying in countless numbers, some of which raised immediately back to their feet and continued their assault, whilst others never rose again.

The exchange lasted for a mere thirty seconds, though it felt like a lifetime. And during that half a minute, the devastation was immense.

Backing off slowly once again, the wolves all panted heavily, many with fresh scars and limps. Their eyes still were set on Vivian, immovable and resolute. Standing still over Kael, unwilling to budge, Vivian too was bleeding in numerous places where she had been caught by fangs and claws, and her breathing was laboured.

A particularly nasty bite on the back of her leg forced her to drop to one knee, where one of the fiends had attempted to hamstring her, and, to all extents, had succeeded. The pain meant nothing to her however, and Vivian simply willed her body to continue, feeding herself with her own power.

The wolves bared their fangs once more, and the fierce young Featherstone prepared for yet another onslaught.

So long as Kael lived, he would be under her protection, and Vivian refused to relent. It would probably mean a fight to the death, but that didn't matter.

She would not yield.

"COME ON!" She screamed at the pack surrounding her, startling them into a frenzy, snapping at her angrily, but hesitant, fearful of her ferocity.

Suddenly then, for some reason, their threats ceased, and Vivian snapped her head round to the side, sensing exactly what had drawn their attention, and fear gripped her senses once more.

She felt then a new set of eyes upon them from amidst the trees, hidden in the shadows. She could see nothing with her eyes, but with her other senses she saw a powerful beast lurking there, just beyond reach.

The wolves snapped and growled threateningly, apparently having forgotten Vivian completely.

Then, all of a sudden, as if from nowhere, hundreds upon thousands of creatures crept into view, moving slowly and silently, but at the same time appearing from absolutely nowhere, encircling the wolves just as they encircled Vivian.

Again, the animals in the huddle were as wide ranging as they'd been before, and they looked on just as imploringly as before.

Abruptly then, for some reason, guilt washed over Vivian, and her anger drained away for a moment.

"I'm sorry." She suddenly pleaded to the crowds of animals all around her. "I don't know what to do."

But the words had barely left her lips, and she scarcely had a moment longer to take in the sight of their spectators, before the enormous beast that she had sensed, at least five times bigger than the biggest of the blackened wolves, came crashing through the trees.

It bellowed an ear splitting roar that Vivian seemed somehow to recognise, and for a second, lost in the sight that she now beheld, Vivian felt time, and indeed everything all around her, come to a complete standstill.

Was this the great bellowing beast that had terrified everybody so?

Vivian's mouth dropped open and her mind emptied completely, shock and disbelief washing over her.

It was only as the enormous red bear grasped the wolf nearest to it, plucking it easily from the ground with its massive jaws, and flung it effortlessly against a tree, killing it outright, that Vivian snapped to her senses.

The great bear looked at her then in a way that tore at Vivian's heart: in a way that she recognised. Its eyes were caring and protective, though focused on the task at hand, hardened by battle.

It even moved like her Red, stalking forwards carefully and precisely, its movements calculated and certain.

It wasn't possible…

Red was dead…

As the huge beast approached her, moving slowly, its eyes trained on the pack, emanating a low, threatening growl from the very back of its throat, Vivian could see its body ripple with muscle, and that its thick muzzle was frosted with grey.

Vivian couldn't even begin to form the question she wanted to ask in her mind, and simply stared numbly at the magnificent animal before her. Having spent many years living with red bears, now, amidst everything, the young Featherstone found herself unable to speak.

Finally, swallowing heavily, Vivian managed a single word.

"R…Red…?"

Suddenly then, at the sound of her voice, the wolves howled and lunged forward, all at once, descending upon the enormous red bear hungrily.

"GO NOW!!" The huge animal roared, its voice so similar to Red's that Vivian could have cried. The only difference was that it was deeper, older, wiser, and much more worn.

After a moment's hesitation, snapping all of a sudden to her senses, Vivian hauled Kael up onto her shoulders, admittedly using quite a bit of sorcery, and fled from the scene off into the vast forest.

She made it but ten paces before she was tackled heavily to the ground, rolling to her back and sending Kael flying, still unconscious. She was immediately pinned down by a vicious, drooling wolf, snarling over her triumphantly.

Suddenly though, whimpering in pain, the wolf was dragged swiftly back, raking at the ground desperately, barely missing Vivian's legs with its slashing claws.

"RUN VIV!" The great red bear roared, crushing the wolf that had attacked her and ripping its throat open with its massive jaws.

Another three wolves jumped on the enormous bear's back then, ripping and tearing at its shoulders terribly.

"VIV, GO!!" The bear bellowed again, desperation tinging the words thrown so urgently, as it writhed to throw the wolves off.

She didn't hesitate this time, grabbing Kael's limp body, his face now white and blanched, and took off into the trees once again, cringing at the sounds of ripping and tearing flesh, crunching and breaking bones, and angry, vicious roars and bellows ringing in her ears.

13

The roars and cries echoing behind her slowly faded and died away amidst yelps and squeals, but Vivian didn't once look back; instead she kept her eyes trained forward and focused, churning her legs furiously.

It was late into the afternoon and the day had begun to cool and chill when Kael awakened from his dazed slumber, stirred by Vivian's thoughts pushing at his.

"W…Wh…What…?" Kael stammered, raising his hand to his throbbing head. He was lay at the back of a stout red pine tree, half covered by a thick shrub.

Vivian crouched attentively at his side, holding his hand in hers. Her eyes were closed and she was clearly lost in deep concentration.

"What happened?" Kael eventually managed, closing his eyes and lying his head back again, for anything else hurt to do, and his vision had started spinning madly.

His words roused Vivian from her searching thoughts and her features relaxed. She breathed deeply and opened her eyes, squinting against the last remaining light of the afternoon streaming down from above, winding its way through the canopy.

"Hold still." She instructed, squeezing his hand tightly. "You've lost a lot of blood."

"Am I alive?" He asked, his tone dubious, and Vivian's reply did little to instil him with fresh confidence.

"Barely." She eventually replied, following a long pause.

"That's why I feel so awful then." He concluded, rather lamely, the faint remnants of a smirk touching his lips.

Vivian did not reply, and Kael sighed deeply, knowing that if he had any chance of survival at all, it lay solely with her.

"How's my leg?" Kael asked then, without opening his eyes. "Is it as bad as it feels?"

"How does it feel?" Was Vivian's immediate reply, not even breaking her concentration as she scanned over Kael's battered and ruined body once again with her mind's eye.

"Like it isn't there…" Kael responded honestly.

"Pretty much…" Vivian agreed in return, her words just as honest.

"I thought so…"

The extent of the damage was not localised to Kael's leg, sadly, and the severe injury had affected his whole body. Vivian could see quite clearly that he'd lost tremendous amounts of blood, and that his heart was under immense pressure, working ten to the dozen, just to try to compensate.

Knowing that they didn't have long, Vivian worked quickly, assessing what to do with what was left of Kael's leg.

Since she had not an abundance of time, nor the leisure of uninterrupted concentration, with the sounds of fighting ever in her ears, she knew she would just have to do her best. Neither time nor concentration would be allowed to her until they returned to civilisation.

She made her decision.

Locating the nerves and veins and arteries in and around Kael's ruined leg, seeing that most of them had been severed, leaving only a few still intact, even if only barely, Vivian set to work.

She repaired those veins and arteries that were leaking the majority of the blood, allowing at least some of the pressure to ease. Then she focused in on the nerves that were causing her Kael so much pain, and cut off the sensation from them completely, at least lifting that barrier too.

Finally, with all the time she had left, Vivian examined the blood rushing through his body - what little of it there was remaining. She studied his cells in detail for a minute or two, seeing their many different types and variations, before, carefully but quickly, multiplying them.

The colour rushed back to Kael's face and she felt him breathe a grateful sigh of relief, as the strain placed upon his heart eased. His heartbeat slowed gradually and, now that the pain was gone, even though his leg was still in a terrible state, his body began to return to more or less normal function.

With her hasty repairs made, knowing of course that they were only temporary, Vivian roused Kael to full consciousness, and his strength was somewhat recovered, enough at least for him to stand on his good leg. He leant quite heavily on Vivian, but he was standing nonetheless. They bound a few stout branches to his bad leg, holding what was left of it in place so that it didn't flail around, and set off back towards Virtus.

Fearful that the wolves would once again find and follow their trail, for it would be near impossible to miss, they hurried on, eating when and where they could, hardly stopping to rest even once.

As they trudged northwards, moving mostly in a kind of awed and terrified silence, Vivian thought of the great red bear that had saved their lives.

She had so believed at first that it was Red, but as soon as she'd heard his voice, it was clear that that was not the case.

But then, if it wasn't her Red, how had it known who she was?

She forced the thoughts from her mind, crushing the pointless hope she had begun to build. Even the tiniest piece wasn't worth.

She knew the truth.

Red was dead.

Or at least she thought she did.

It took them several days, travelling at their wearied but relentless pace, to reach Jared's southern farmstead, entrusting their safety to luck and to fate and to the great red bear that had saved them. When they finally arrived, they were met, understandably, with concerned looks and worried words.

"Vivian! Kael!" Jared yelled, rushing over to them, their return having been highlighted to everyone by one of his farmhands.

Kael looked much worse for wear, but he was at least alive. Vivian too looked weak and drained, but the determination to save Kael was clear in her eyes.

"What happened!?" Jared asked automatically, but Vivian waved his question off.

"There's no time for that now!" Vivian instructed. "I need shelter, water, and food, now!"

Her words were sharp and to the point, and one look at Kael's ruined leg told Jared all that he needed to know. He set about immediately issuing instructions to the first farmhands he laid his eyes upon.

"Water. Food. Clear the southern cottage." He ordered, pointing at a different person with each directive. "Vivian, follow Ciara." He told the young, exhausted Featherstone, indicating the young girl he had just spoken to as he did so.

Vivian nodded and she and Kael hurried hastily after the young girl, her face pale and her bottom lip quivering. Ciara had taken one look at Kael's horrible injury and her stomach had turned, but she did not argue, knowing that the young man badly needed aid.

Without uttering another word to anybody, Vivian and a few others helped Kael to the southernmost cottage of the farmstead, taking him immediately inside and laying him on the bed.

The cottage was well furnished and clearly regularly used, but none of that mattered, and Vivian glossed over the details, instead turning her attention immediately to Kael's injury, knowing that he needed her help, and he needed it now.

This could wait no longer.

She steadied herself, pushing her own fatigue from her mind, and ignoring as best she could the fact that the wolves were probably still close behind them, about to attack the farmstead at any moment.

With a deep breath, her hands trembling slightly, Vivian set to work.

She delved yet again with her mind's eye into Kael's ruined leg, scanning over his entire body as she did so, seeing that whilst he was alive, he was very weak, and some of the blood she had replaced had yet again been lost, leaving his heart under much stress.

Some parts of his leg had begun to heal themselves, though they were all at terrible angles, and so were healing in the wrong directions. Whilst, on the other hand, others had received no blood at all, because they had been so badly severed, and so consequently were dying, or already dead, black and rotting.

Vivian remembered the few times she'd healed herself, and that had, in comparison to this, been much easier. She'd been able to feel what she was doing, stopping and continuing as and when she knew it felt right. But in healing Kael she had no such luxury, for he was barely conscious, and she simply had to do the best she could, relying solely on her instincts.

Hours passed by, dragging laboriously on, ticking their minutes past seemingly as slowly as they could possibly manage.

Vivian's concentration wavered not even an inch during that time, for she was as focused as she'd ever been in her entire life. Her thoughts were bent solely upon fusing the ruined remnants of Kael's knee back together.

She repaired muscle and skin and tendons and ligaments, sewing them all precariously into position, desperately trying to hold them still as she moulded his knee back into something of a workable shape. The intricacy of the work Vivian was attempting forced her to rely heavily on the shape and design of Kael's remaining good knee, for his left leg had at least been spared from the terrible trap.

Mirroring and copying the other, Vivian shaped and sculpted his right knee continuously, filling the joint with fluids and capsules, stitching the tendons and ligaments back onto the muscles, and repairing the soft tissue around it as best as she could.

Finally, when the knee was in the best shape Vivian could possibly manage, she set about once again replacing the blood that Kael had lost, though she knew his body would take care of anything she missed itself too, hopefully…

Eventually, exhausted from her efforts, Vivian let relax her concentration, and she slumped to the floor, breathing heavily and closing her eyes for a minute or two.

Kael was weak, but he was alive, and his knee seemed healed. He had yet to make use of it of course, and that would be the real test, but at least for now it was linked to the rest of his body again.

"Vivian…?" The young man managed weakly, propping himself slowly up onto one elbow, his head spinning precariously.

"Kael…" She replied, just as weakly, and with a meek chuckle, happy to see he had come round to consciousness so quickly. "How do you feel?" She asked, sitting up and taking his hand instinctively.

"About as good as you do by the looks of it." He replied, laughing gingerly. "How long have I been out for?"

"You've been in and out for a few days." Vivian told him honestly. "It took that long to get back here."

"Feels like hours…" Kael mused. "Not days…"

"I didn't know if you were going to make it…" Vivian admitted, her voice catching as a lump formed in her throat.

Kael looked at her very seriously then, levelling his eyes into hers in a way Vivian had never seen.

"Of course I did." He told her. "I had a reason to."

Vivian opened her mouth to reply, but no words came out, for she didn't know what to say. She closed it again, unable to speak, for the lump in her throat had spread to her stomach, and it felt filled to the brim with butterflies.

Her feelings churned in the same way, as they stared into each other's eyes in silence for what felt like hours, but what was probably in fact only seconds.

Then, unable to resist any longer, Vivian clasped her hands about Kael's cheeks, feeling their fresh flooding warmth in her palms, and pulled him into a fervent kiss. He pulled her up from the floor, twisting to sit as he did so, all in the same movement, and kissed her back with passion fiery and longing.

As Kael lifted Vivian, holding her close, she wrapped her legs around his waist, and her thumbs found their way to the sides of his lips. Not once did they separate, and their kiss grew only more intense and adoring as they pulled each other closer, hearts and hands and lips throbbing madly, desperately.

Finally, gasping for breath, their chests heaving, Vivian and Kael released from their fraught kiss. Kael ran his hands firmly up her back, never wanting to let her go, and Vivian clutched at him for all she was worth, having never felt like this in her life.

Vivian looked deeply into Kael's eyes then, as she rested her head and nose gently on his, her breaths shuddering with frantic excitement.

Lost in their own emotions then, they would likely have stayed there indefinitely, paying no heed whatsoever to the world around them, had it not been for what happened next.

A shrill cry reached their ears, followed by a flurry of screams, penetrating and destroying the feeling they were holding so closely between them.

Though it pained her to do so, for every inch of her existence wished to stay in that moment with Kael, Vivian tore her eyes from his and scrambled to the door. She reached it not a moment too soon, and as she yanked it open she laid eyes upon one of Jared's farmhands, racing towards her.

"Miss Featherstone!" He exclaimed, gasping for breath as he ran. "In the woods! Please! They're here!!"

"I'm coming!" She told him immediately, though she cast a fleeting, longing and disheartened glance back to Kael, seeing that he was already on his feet and pulling on his boots, moving very gingerly on his leg.

"Go arm yourself!" He ordered the young farmhand, his voice stern and full of purpose. "We're on our way!"

The young man nodded and turned instantly on his heel, barely breaking his stride, and continuing running in the opposite direction.

Vivian turned back to Kael.

"No, Kael." She said, her voice firm and unwavering in her words. "You need to rest."

"I'm fine." He told her simply, still gathering his things and making for the door, leaning on the wall as he moved, grimacing with pain.

"You have to rest!" Vivian repeated.

But Kael was having none of it.

He limped over to her, his leg clearly still having some healing of its own to do, and he wrapped his hands about her waist and pulled her close, kissing her passionately once again.

Finally he broke the embrace and intertwined his fingers in Vivian's.

"We both need rest, but neither of us have a choice."

Vivian found she could only nod in reply, unable to locate her tongue.

He was right.

And so, without another word, they headed out of the door together, making as quickly as they could for the barn, and for the tree line, and, undoubtedly, for the onslaught that awaited them.

They were both wearied and fatigued, and they struggled to focus as the late afternoon sun dipped lower and lower towards the horizon in the clear sky above. But, nonetheless, Vivian and Kael held themselves resolutely, their willingness and determination filtering out to the men and women all around them: farmhands and villagers, armed with pitchforks and makeshift blades and clubs, pots and pans, all awaiting the blitzing attack headed straight for them.

Dragging themselves to the very front of the massive party, spread out parallel to the rustling and wavering tree line, they prepared to fight, readying their own weapons.

Kael held a small knife in one hand, and a slightly larger short sword in the other. Vivian had no weapons, but instead kept her eyes trained on the woodlands laid out before them.

The forest was the place she had once called home; in fact, it was probably still the closest thing she had to a home, and it pained her that now she feared it so.

"Steady!" Vivian sounded, her voice reaching the ears of her people: the very souls she was trying so hard to protect.

"They're coming!" Jared yelled, pointing through a slight gap in the trees.

Barely even visible, a trunk knocked heavily, shaking the branches above, and a looming shadow slipped between the dark seas of trees.

"Look out!" Another voice shouted, spreading panic through Vivian's ranks. But something tugged at the back of her mind, and suddenly, she knew better.

"HOLD! STEADY!" She commanded, her voice barking with such authority that no one dared argue.

She approached the trees slowly, her defensive posture faltering, and all traces of her fear gradually faded away with each step.

"Viv…" Kael started, wondering what in the world she was doing.

But then, suddenly, enormous and looming from the shadows of the trees, as if slipping and detaching from the very trunks themselves, the great red bear materialised from the tree line, shifting his massive bulk easily and silently, though he limped heavily on his front left leg.

The young Featherstone felt her worry and her apprehension drop away completely then, and all those standing behind her too let their guards lower slightly, though not entirely.

All had heard the stories of the monstrous bear that Vivian had returned to Virtus with, and that the Greystones had taken his life, and, in return, her wrath had been dreadful. They were not about to make the same mistake.

The great bear stood for a moment, staring intently at Vivian, his curious eyes examining her own, before finally, after a minute or two, he seemed satisfied.

He was wounded, clearly, Vivian could see that, but even though fresh blood trickled down his massive torso and legs, the magnificent bear seemed not in the slightest bit phased. At least as big as Red had been, if not even larger, the great beast walked straight up to her then, and dropped its massive head down to the height of Vivian's.

The animal's greyed and silvery muzzle moved in the same strange and mesmerising manner that Red's had done, and even as he spoke, the similarities between them were so obvious to Vivian that she couldn't quite believe it.

"Vivian Featherstone." The great bear said then, not so much in a question, but instead more in the way of a formal greeting: an absolute certainty.

He knew who she was, without a shadow of a doubt.

"I am." She replied simply, nodding her head to the beautiful animal, tears brimming in her eyes.

"My name is Emerson." The he told her, speaking plainly.

Vivian nodded in reply, unable to speak, but somehow at the same time knowing what was coming next.

"I'm Red's father."

14

"Are we safe?" Vivian asked, pouring her eyes into Emerson's, still desperately trying to process what she was hearing.

"They are some way away." The great red bear, Emerson, Red's father, assured her. His voice was gentle and understanding, as Red and Clover's had always been, and he spoke with the certain surety that only the red bears had ever possessed.

"What happened?" Vivian asked then, though, in hindsight, she realised that the answer to that question was probably an obvious one. Nonetheless though, Emerson answered her with the patience of the Redwoods themselves.

"It's not the first time I've fought to defend my home." He replied honestly, shrugging his massive shoulders, though the leg he limped on hindered his movement noticeably.

Vivian nodded understandingly, not once taking her eyes from the huge bear before her, scanning over his fur, blood stained and ragged, somewhat longingly.

He cocked his head curiously to one side, in exactly the same way that Red used to, Vivian noted, the sight of it forcing her to choke back tears.

"May I?" She finally asked, and he nodded his vast head understandingly, seeming to know exactly what she meant, without the need for an explanation.

She took a few cautious steps towards the great bear; having been denied this for so long, as she stretched her hand out towards him, it shook noticeably and her breaths grew shallow and sharp.

The whole thing almost overwhelmed the still young Featherstone.

Emerson, undoubtedly Red's father, spoke and sounded like her dear Red, looked like him, moved like him…

How had she never known?

Vivian's fingers reached his thick, warm fur, soft against her skin, and she ran her hand through it blissfully, feeling beneath the warmth his strength and his resolution. The sensation was magical, for it was something Vivian had done daily, without even thinking, for so long, when she'd lived with Red. So now, having been denied it for so long, the feeling was both so alien and so familiar, that it stirred happiness inside of her tenfold.

"Jared!" Vivian called then, raising her voice and looking over her shoulder. She needn't have shouted however, for the elderly farmstead owner had slowly been making his way through the crowds to her, and was stood barely six feet behind her and Kael.

"Yes, Miss Vivian…" He responded, his voice shuddering a little, though he was of course overjoyed that the bear seemed to be friend rather than foe.

"I need food, and water." She stated simply, turned her gaze back to her hand running through the thick fur she had longed to touch again for so long. "Emerson has come a long way. He needs to rest."

It was only as the dark of the night had begun to settle for the evening that Vivian finally finished healing Emerson's numerous wounds. Beneath his thick fur they had been difficult to see with her naked eyes, but with her other senses, Vivian had clearly seen the horrible extent of the damage the wolves had delivered upon her dear Red's father.

"Thank you Vivian." The great bear said simply, sat in the comparable warmth and shelter of the partly desolated barn.

Many of the holes and damages had been boarded up, and as a flurry of showers and storms set in for the night, Vivian, Emerson and Kael were all grateful for the shelter from the elements.

Vivian had explained in quite some detail to Jared and his farmhands that Emerson was most definitely a friend, and that he had saved them in the forest from the wolves that had been killing their cattle.

As Vivian told them of what had happened, and that they wouldn't have made it back if it hadn't been for the great red bear, their awe and respect for the animal grew tenfold.

The three of them sat in silence for some time as Emerson ate, tearing his way through several very large chunks of meat that Jared had instructed be brought through for him.

The barn was lit by a few covered oil lamps, placed here and there around the large space, and Vivian and Kael sat in the silhouette of the great bear as he ate and drank. They sat close, feeding off each other's warmth and holding hands tightly, their fingers intertwined, watching Emerson with fascination.

This was a new captivation for Kael, for he had never seen such a sight, even during all his weeks and months travelling south from his old home. And for Vivian, though of course she had lived with the red bears, she had been deprived of their company for so long, that she simply revelled in Emerson's company.

"What's going on Emerson?" She finally asked, when he had finished feeding. "Why did the wolves attack us?"

The great bear pushed aside what remained of the carcass he had been devouring, nudging it out of the way with his snout, and sighed heavily, settling down on the floor and looking at Vivian with a very level gaze.

"You sensed them." He said then, his tone very matter of fact. "I know you did."

"Yes…" Vivian replied, her voice dropping low as if embarrassed.

"You were right." He encouraged her. "Don't hide from the fact. What did you sense?"

Vivian remained silent for a minute or two, but eventually she spoke up again, as Kael looked at her inquisitively, not knowing what the huge bear was getting at.

"The plague…" Vivian whispered. "The Greystones…"

Emerson nodded, but this time it was he that did not reply. Instead, he waited patiently for Vivian to begin to piece things together.

"But I've never sensed them before…" Vivian thought aloud. "Not once since I killed the Grey. So why now?" She mused.

Again, Emerson shrugged his massive shoulders.

"I don't know." He admitted. "I've been watching them for a long time now, ever since you killed the Grey in fact." He explained. "They've been keeping themselves hidden from you, until now. Now they seem to want your attention. I think that's why they started attacking the cattle…"

"But why?" Vivian urged. "Why now?" But Emerson shook his head.

"I don't know." He admitted again.

"Perhaps they've been preparing?" Kael suggested, piping up from his somewhat withdrawn silence. "Perhaps they've been gathering their strength, and now they want to flush you out and kill you?" He suggested, before adding a final comment. "And they nearly managed it…"

"Perhaps…" Emerson conceded.

"Where have they come from?" Vivian asked then.

"I'm sorry Vivian." Emerson apologised then, speaking very openly and honestly. "I really don't know. I only know what I have to know, just the same as you."

But then, veering off topic somewhat, cutting straight through to the line of questioning that was really bothering her, Vivian cast another query at the great red bear.

"Where have you been, Emerson? Why haven't I ever met you before? Why didn't Clover ever mention you?" The questions tumbled from Vivian's tongue in a single, flowing breath, without giving Emerson chance to answer even one of them.

Vivian had realised, for some reason, that it had never been something she'd considered when living with Red and Clover. She'd never even though to ask, though now it seemed an all too obvious question, for Clover had never even mentioned the notion of Red's father.

Emerson sighed deeply, and Vivian could see immediately that, not only had he expected this question, but also that it pained him deeply.

Suddenly she felt immensely guilty, realising in that instant that it had never been the great red bear's decision to leave, but instead that he'd had no choice in the matter.

And sure enough, Emerson's response confirmed Vivian's suspicions, for his words were laden with the pain of loss and responsibility.

"I had no choice." He said first, cutting straight to the point. "The Redwoods told me that I needed to remain separate from my family, for there were some very important things that absolutely had to happen. They told me that those things couldn't come to pass if I remained with Clover and Red…"

Immediately, at the mention of their names, Emerson's voice thickened heavily, and he struggled to fight back tears. Vivian had never seen such a majestic creature cry. Even Red had not cried when his mother had died, and the sight tore at the young Featherstone's heart terribly.

"Why?" She asked then. "What had to happen?"

"I don't know." Emerson admitted then, though Vivian sensed he was not being entirely truthful, but instead that his response was designed to protect her.

It didn't work.

She knew then, instinctively, amidst everything, that the reason was altogether to do with her. A massive wave of guilt surged through Vivian, knowing that, for whatever reason, it was because of her that Emerson had been denied a life of love and happiness with his family. She had taken that from him, and then, as if that wasn't enough, she had allowed his soul mate and his son to die at the hands of the Greystones.

Vivian's heart felt suddenly heavy with regret and sorrow, weighing her down like a stone in her chest.

"I'm sorry Emerson…" She managed to choke, her voice welling up suddenly.

"Please don't apologise." He pleaded of her then, seeing Vivian's revelation in her haunted eyes. "You are wrong." He told her, his voice even a little stern. "It's not your fault. It was never your choice, just as it wasn't mine. Had I not separated from my Clover and my Red…"

At those words Vivian's barriers fell and tears began to streak openly down her cheeks, but Emerson continued nonetheless.

"Then you may as well have died at the hands of the Greystones all those years ago, when you were just a girl, for things would have played out very differently, and the world would likely have been lost to the Greystone plague."

Vivian nodded, understanding his words, though she sensed he was simply offering her his best guesswork.

It did little to soften the crucifying blow of her guilt however, and that terrible feeling settled deeply inside of her, and would remain there for the rest of her days.

"I have no regret." Emerson told her then. "Sorrow, perhaps." He admitted. "But no regret."

"But the plague is still here." Vivian managed, composing herself as best she could. "What was the point if I still didn't manage to kill it!?"

But Emerson was prepared for that question also, and the long, hard stare he gave Vivian then spoke volumes, and was through and through the look of a parent.

"I am not the one to answer that question." He told her. "I don't have the answer, and you know it."

Vivian nodded meekly, knowing she'd been out of line. Her question was not meant for Emerson; it was meant for the Redwoods.

Suddenly then, rising to his feet in a swift, deadly movement, Emerson let from his throat a deep, terrifying growl, so similar to Red's that it took Vivian back years into her memory, even as her body responded to the sound.

"What is it!?" She hissed through clenched teeth, springing to her feet, glancing all around, keeping her voice low.

The heavily falling rain above hammered against the roof of the tattered barn so loudly that it had blocked out the sound of their entire conversation, but still Vivian and Emerson spoke in hushed whispers.

Kael immediately raced for the barricaded barn door, and removed the bar from across it. Hauling the heavy barricade to the side, he pushed the doors open, creaking and wailing on their rusty hinges.

Without wasting another second, knowing without the need for words what was happening, the three of them took off into the night, soaked in an instant by the heavy raindrops, yelling at the tops of their voices, rousing the farmstead once again for battle. The falling rain barraged Vivian's face harshly as she tore through the darkness, Kael beside her to her left, with only a slight limp now, and Emerson to her right, his great, looming silhouette terrifying in the night.

"GET BACK!" Emerson roared, seeing the farmhands they had alerted approaching the tree line, weapons at the ready, blinded by the night.

They withdrew automatically, fearful not only of what lay within the trees, but also of Emerson's powerful approach. He pounded the ground with his great strides as he ran, tearing up vast chunks of earth and mud. His fur was dripping from the rain and clung to his huge, muscular, hulking body.

Above the heavy pounding of the rain, slamming against the cold ground, the array of howls and baying cries reached Vivian's ears, ripping through the air over and between the trees.

They had but mere seconds before the black shadowy beasts exploded from the undergrowth, disguised amidst the darkness beneath the heavily fortified clouds and rain.

When the wolves attacked, launching from the trees with renewed vigour and malice, Vivian lit them up with great streaks of flames, unquenchable even in the thundering rainfall, allowing the farmhands at least the chance to see the monsters they were supposed to be fighting.

Cries and yelps and screams of pain echoed out then, as the humans and the plague ridden beasts clashed. Emerson bellowed a terrifying and earth-shaking roar, and began to methodically crush every monster he came to face.

Vivian too dealt her own devastation, and Kael darted in and out, left and right, his replenished leg holding up well, swiping and attacking here and there, always striking the most vulnerable and vital parts of his enemies. His hard life had moulded him well, making his wiry muscles strong and his reflexes sharp, even following his injury.

The battle raged on.

The freezing cold rain continued to fall, saturating everything until finally it had run its full course. The clouds eventually lifted to reveal a full moon, shining its reflected light down upon the battlefield, strewn with fresh bodies and blood.

But the tables seemed to be turning, and though the plague infected wolves had begun to fall in great numbers, more and more of their kind poured from the woodlands, their ranks seeming to swell limitlessly, overwhelming Vivian and Kael and Emerson and Jared and his men.

It wasn't long at all before they seemed fated to lose, their defences being brutally and methodically ripped to shreds.

Then however, and not for the first time, something very strange happened.

Everything seemed to slow for Vivian, as if time itself was grinding to a halt. Even amidst the fighting and clawing and biting snarls of their enemies then, she felt eyes upon them.

She glanced around, her eyes wide in the new light of the moon, and saw hundreds upon thousands of animals in the tree line, watching and listening, looking on eagerly, waiting.

Instinctively, and entirely without thinking, Vivian threw a desperate request out to them, asking, begging, pleading for their help. And then, amazingly, as if she'd expected her efforts to be futile, they responded.

The armies of the Redwood Forest itself poured out from the trees then, turning the tide of the battle once more, overwhelming the plague ridden beasts and engulfing them almost entirely.

Vivian's mouth fell open when she realised what she'd just done, as wolves and bears and foxes and even deer streamed out from the trees, kicking and screaming and clawing and slashing at the wolves, churning the ground into a muddied bloodbath.

And so the fighting would have continued, probably long on through the night, had it not been interrupted…

A terrible roaring screech echoed out high above them then, ten times louder than even Emerson could have possibly managed.

All heads turned, casting their gazes high up into the sky, above the sea of Redwoods, illuminated so by the dazzling moonlight.

The sight they beheld was accompanied by the sound of tremendous flapping wings, and the silhouette of a black, devil like figure, somehow even darker than the night itself, loomed overhead, blocking the light from the moon and from the few peeking stars, engulfing everything.

"THAT'S IT!" Jared cried, pointing up and the menacing silhouette, gripped by icy fear. "THAT'S THE SOUND!"

Clearly Vivian had been wrong. The roaring screeches that the farmhands had all described had not been Emerson after all, she suddenly realised.

But her epiphany came too late.

From high above, swooping down in a long, graceful arc, clear to all of them even in the dim light of the night, the demon was illuminated by the moonshine. The enormous creature, silhouetted against the glittering blanket above, easily five times the size of Emerson, was a dragon.

Fear seized Vivian for a moment, immobilising her, for she had always assured herself, rightly or wrongly, that such things were only the beasts of fables and fairy tales.

Clearly she had been wrong, as the devastating power of the creature above then became all too apparent.

The monstrous black dragon swept down, skimming the tips of the trees as it did so, screeching deafeningly out into the night. Vivian could even feel the hatred of the beast, a menace and lust for revenge instilled within it by the Greystone's plague, greater than that of all the plague ridden wolves combined.

The wolves immediately fled back into the forest, though at first glance it seemed to Vivian that their retreat was tactical, planned, rather than created out of fear, for they did not seem afraid in the slightest.

"GET DOWN!" Vivian suddenly screamed, coming finally to her senses, realising suddenly the danger they were in as the terrible serpent swept overhead. She threw herself to the ground and was followed closely by Kael. He landed right by her side, bleeding profusely from his left arm.

Emerson however, was not given the opportunity, and he was a much more obvious target than the humans. The dragon snatched at him with its massive talon like claws as it swept in, monstrous and powerful, plucking the huge bear from the ground seemingly without effort, digging its claws deep into his sides.

The great red bear roared in pain and struggled desperately to free himself. But the reptilian beast, taken straight from myth and fantasy, was simply too strong, and the more Emerson struggled, the deeper the monster's claws sank.

Vivian leapt to her feet and screamed uselessly after them, as the dragon took off again into the night, carrying the poor flailing bear with it, blotting the light from the moon once more as it flew off into the distance over the vast forest.

A hauntingly familiar feeling of loss, and a surge or regret, hit Vivian then, knocking the wind and the fight from her as if she'd just run headlong into a brick wall. Her knees buckled as she tried uselessly to run after them, the strength and the fight stolen from her, and despair overwhelmed her.

The great red bear, his struggles fading swiftly, along with his life, disappeared over the great ocean of blood red pines, and was carried off towards the peaks and mountains far to the south.

15

Some people were screaming and shouting, whilst others remained stood still and unable to move, shell-shocked. Then from the rear some began to run, fleeing back to their homes, whilst others had already locked and bolted their doors, far ahead of them.

Kael climbed slowly to his feet, grunting as the weight on his injured arm and his still not quite fully healed leg sent shots of fresh pain through his system.

The sound beside her rallied Vivian's focus back, shocking her suddenly into action.

"JARED!" She shouted immediately, the sound of her voice penetrating the darkness sharply.

"Miss Featherstone!" He replied in an instant, rushing to her side, limping slightly himself.

"I need everybody looking for wounded." She instructed. "Get everyone who's still alive to take the injured back to the cottages and give them treatment."

"What about…Wh…The…" Jared stammered, glancing nervously up above the trees, unable to say the word.

"Forget it." Vivian told him. "I will deal with it. Do as I have asked."

He nodded curtly and took off without another word, seemingly grateful to have been given a task that did not involve fighting a dragon.

The next hour or so was devoted entirely to searching the battlefield for any who were still alive, and then rushing them off to find shelter and give them medical aid. Vivian always kept one eye on the tree line however, all too wary that the wolves could return at any time.

She worked frantically, not stopping even for a moment.

It was all she could do to keep her mind from wandering towards thoughts of Emerson, and of the great, hollow cavern that had once again opened up afresh within her very heart.

Finally, after having scoured the waterlogged fields and sifted through the bloody remains of friend and foe alike, Vivian summoned Jared once more.

"I think that's all of them…" The very weary farmstead owner reported, the look in his eyes something of a haunted one.

"Good." Vivian replied, her tone authoritative and aged. "Get everyone back to their homes, and make sure that anyone who needs care gets it."

"What of the dragon?" He asked again then, plucking up the courage to utter the unspeakable word at long last.

Vivian remained silent for a moment, churning his question over in her mind; but as much as she thought on it, somewhat resentfully, she knew exactly what she had to do.

"I felt something in the dragon, and in the wolves; something that I never expected to feel again." She admitted, sighing deeply and glancing up and the moonlit night sky. Many more stars had appeared now and they danced across the black ocean above without a care.

"You felt something?" Jared asked, confused.

"I sensed the Greystones." Vivian told him then, her words blunt and to the point. "Their plague lives on in those poor creatures." She sighed again as she spoke, only this time she exhaled with great sorrow.

"But, how can that be?" Jared asked, knowing as all did that Vivian had banished their evil when she had returned to Virtus. "I thought you killed them all?"

"I did." Vivian began to explain. "You're right, but their evil still lingers in these poor creatures." As she spoke she swept her gaze across the bloodbath that was laid out all around them, and Vivian suddenly felt very guilty, about a lot of different things. "It's all that's left of them."

Jared nodded but, not knowing what to say, didn't reply. Instead, Kael placed a gentle and assuring hand on Vivian's shoulder, and smiled as reassuringly as he could manage.

"I need you to keep your people hidden." Vivian continued, looking very seriously at Jared. "I need you to keep them safe."

"Where are you going!? What are you going to do!?" He suddenly exclaimed, terrified at the thought of another attack without their so called saviour there to defend them.

"I'm going back to Featherstone Keep. I have to find out how to kill it." Vivian told him, unwillingly admitting with that statement that she actually had no idea what to do, and was simply resorting to that which she knew and was familiar.

"Can't you just use your power?" He pleaded. "You killed the Grey! You can't leave us to die! Can't you just kill it!?"

The desperation in the poor farmstead owner's voice choked Vivian, but she knew now what she had to do, and she wouldn't leave them in danger. It wasn't these poor people that the creatures wanted.

She had felt their lust for her before, and now it was no different.

"I won't let them hurt your people anymore." Vivian told him, but he would not listen.

"They've been attacking us for months!" He blurted. "And now since you've come to help us two dozen more have died!" Jared caught his tongue there, knowing he had overstepped the mark, terrified at what the consequences might be.

But Vivian did not respond. She only smiled ruefully, knowing his words were only the truth.

"I know, Jared." She eventually admitted. "And that's exactly why I have to leave. The Greystones have wanted me for my entire life. Ever since the day I was born, they've sought nothing but to claim me, to kill me. They will never be happy until they have me."

"I'm sorry…" Jared started, but Kael cut him off.

"Vivian…" He interrupted. "What are you going to do?" He asked.

There was a heavy pause that hung for a moment, as realisation dawned in Kael's eyes.

"But…You can't…No!" He didn't even give her chance to reply, following her trail of thought before she'd even had chance to reveal it.

"Now they've found me, they will follow me." Vivian explained. She knew that wasn't entirely the truth, but she was simplifying it for Jared, trying to reassure him. "So I will lead them away. I will lead them back to Featherstone Keep, and nobody can follow me."

Even as Vivian spoke, knowing she had to go back to Featherstone Keep, she didn't have a clue why. She only knew that it was her only remaining option. She had to get away from civilisation, and there was simply nowhere else to go. She couldn't bear the thought of more innocent lives being lost.

Jared abruptly changed the subject then, suddenly switching topics.

"Did you summon the animals from the Redwoods?" He asked. "Did you ask them to fight for us?"

"Yes." Vivian replied simply, though in her mind she finished her sentence with 'I think, but I don't know how.'

"How?" He asked then, as if he had read her thoughts, but Vivian's expression told him not to dwell on such things.

"It doesn't matter." She told him. "All that matters is that your people are safe now."

Jared nodded his head, knowing instinctively that she could say no more on the matter. Instead, he politely excused himself, apologising again for his outburst, and left Vivian in Kael's company, saying that he would allow her time to prepare for her departure.

As she watched the farmstead owner fade away and disappear into the night, moving slowly towards the collection of cottages, she couldn't help but sigh, wishing that their conversation had gone better. But there was nothing she could do about it now. The most important thing was to protect her people, and to remove this threat, once and for all.

She had much work to do.

Back at the cottage that had been allocated for Kael's recovery, he and Vivian sat at the wooden kitchen table eating a thick stew that had been brought round to them by one of the farmstead's kitchen staff. It was a concoction of vegetables and chewy chunks of meat, and though neither of them felt particularly hungry, they forced it down regardless, knowing they needed to eat.

The room was lighted by a single candle that stood on a tray, sat between them on the table, and the silence was an eerie one, for following all of the chaos so far that night, it seemed most unnatural.

"You know I'm coming with you." Kael told Vivian then, seemingly from nowhere, shattering the silence with his statement.

"You can't Kael…" Vivian started, but she hadn't the heart to finish.

Her head told her the undoubted, logical truth: that even with all her power, what Vivian was planning would be dangerous, and if Kael came, he would surely die. Her heart however, telling an altogether different story, yearned for him to accompany her, and the mere thought of separating from him again ripped pain in Vivian's chest unbearably.

Such a decision is always a difficult one to make, but indeed forms the very basis of who we are.

"Why?" He asked then, seeming to encompass all that she had just thought with that one simple word.

Vivian decided that he would accept nothing less than the truth, and neither should he have done.

"Because I can't bear the thought of losing you." She admitted honestly, opening up to the young man in a way she would never have expected.

"You won't lose me." He assured her, and though his words were of course meant to be genuine, he had no way of knowing that for sure.

"You can't say that." Vivian said, shaking her head.

"But…"

"BUT NOTHING!!" Vivian suddenly screamed, rising to her feet and knocking their empty bowls flying across the floor, clattering against the stone.

Tears streamed openly down her cheeks and her shoulders shook and shuddered from forcing back intermittent sobs.

"My mother and father are gone! Red's gone! Clover's gone! And now even Emerson's gone! I hadn't even known him a day!!" She cried, dropping her hands to the table to support her crumbling frame, her shaking legs failing her.

Kael rushed to Vivian's side and she fell helplessly into his arms, choking and sobbing uncontrollably, her years of pain and anguish coming flooding out all in one terrible burst.

"I…I…I can't…I…" Vivian attempted, but she was unable to speak, and Kael comforted her and held her close.

For some time they remained there until, finally, seeing she was exhausted, Kael carried the young Featherstone through from the kitchen and into the bedroom. Laying her down on the bed, her cries eventually having subsided, he ran his hand gently across her back, still shaking slightly.

"I can't lose you…" Vivian whispered in the darkness, for now there was no candle to light the room.

"I can't lose you either." Kael replied. "That's why I don't want you to go alone."

For that response Vivian had no reply.

So, instead, she rolled onto her back and lifted her hand to Kael face in the blackness, stroking his cheek tenderly as he sat on her bedside. They stayed there for a moment, not so much looking at each other, for neither of them could see. Instead, they simply savoured that moment in each other's company, for those fleeting chances to be with the ones we love so dearly do not come around very often: certainly not often enough.

Kael leaned down to kiss her then, touching his lips to Vivian's slowly and carefully, as if that was exactly where they belonged. He pursed his lips open against hers and slowly let them shut, as if they were designed to be together, and the feeling took Vivian's breath away.

She reached up and ran her hands through Kael's hair, pulling him close and not letting him go even once.

Before she knew it, Vivian had rolled him over her and they lay together on the bed, lips and fingers locked. She ripped Kael's shirt up off over his head, running her hands over his chest and back as she did so, and in an instant he too pulled her clothes away, flinging them off in the darkness.

He held her tightly, kissed her passionately, his lips exploring her body, and Vivian tore the few clothes Kael had left from him, tossing them away, not caring where they went.

Vivian wrapped her legs around his and pulled him as close as she could manage, arching her back with the feeling, throbbing, kissing and biting his lips feverishly, frantic and longing.

The night passed by in a blur for Vivian and Kael, unaware of the passage of time during those eventful hours, their hearts raced and their breaths were short and sharp and loud. Bound tightly together, rolling over and over almost uncontrollably in the darkness, Vivian had never felt so loved.

She had never felt so alive.

When the dark hours of the early morning had finally passed, just as the sun crept over the horizon, illuminating the horror of the night before, Vivian breathed deeply the cold air, sharp as razors in her lungs. She looked up at the light blue sky, clear and empty with not a cloud to be seen.

Nothing was simple anymore. Nothing had been simple for a long time.

Life in the Redwoods with Clover and Red had been, but besides that, everything else seemed horribly complicated.

Last night was perhaps the only exception.

She had not slept at all, and the thing that stuck in her mind the most, even still, was her overwhelming desire for Kael, in every sense of the word. Her feelings for him were deeper than ever, and she had never known such a thing.

So powerful, it filled Vivian completely, almost to the point of bursting, or so it felt.

She adored him.

She loved him.

That much at least was clear at least.

"Hurry up you idiot." A voice sounded from round behind the cottage. Vivian's breath caught in her throat and she ducked to the side, dipping out of sight just in time to see two men round the corner, moving quickly and crouching low, talking in hushed whispers.

"I'm coming Zander…" The second man whispered submissively, hurrying along.

"Well you're taking too bloody long!" Zander, replied harshly. "All those animals that were here last night, we're bound to have got some, and I don't want them to go rotten just because you're a useless moron!"

The second man, Astley, did not reply then, but instead just hurried along behind his openly abusive companion.

Vivian watched with cold, dead eyes as the two men, the two poachers, raced off across the battle field of the night before, and slipped away into the woodlands. She had followed them once before, but had never come across them again since then.

The Redwoods Rise and Fall

They had given her the slip many times before now, forcing her to leave them as unfinished business.

Their being here surely wasn't by chance, and if they were here, it was undoubtedly their trap that had destroyed Kael's leg.

With a heavy heart, set in the unbreakable stone that is cold-blooded revenge and murder, Vivian's night of love was all but forgotten, as is all too often the way, replaced by a lust that was both insatiable and unprecedented.

She set off after the two men into the Redwoods, her path lighted by the early morning sun streaming down upon her, filtering its way through the canopy of branches and leaves above.

Her mind was made up; it had not been a difficult decision.

This time she would not be left empty handed, and her intentions were not innocent by any stretch of the imagination.

In fact, they were quite the opposite.

Malicious would not have been a strong enough word to describe Vivian's thoughts at that moment.

She simply hoped that no one crossed her path until her work was done, for she would surely not rest until there was fresh blood on her hands.

16

Though the sun sat brightly in the sky, it was still low, and the remaining cold of the night had not yet passed. There was a chill breeze that picked up and dropped periodically, whipping in and out of the trunks and branches and leaves, stirring them into a frenzy above Vivian's head as she stalked her way through the trees.

Just as the leaves about her feet danced and skipped, their wet faces sparkling and shining red from the night's heavy rainfall, Vivian's emotions stirred too, lashing around inside her chest endlessly. Just as when she had killed the Grey, not to mention all the others that had fallen to her heavy hand and terrible wrath, Vivian's desperate lust for vengeance, her ceaseless desire to kill, left her feeling empty and unfulfilled.

Kael had perhaps temporarily subdued that great chasm, during their blissful night together. But now that had seemingly all been forgotten, and Vivian's focus had shifted entirely.

Her revenge was not entirely self-focused however, for it had of course been Kael that had suffered the bear trap. But nonetheless, this was not how Kael would have responded, and Vivian knew it.

This lust for murder was hers, and hers alone.

It was perhaps half an hour or so later, after having begun her deathly task amidst the vast woodlands, that Vivian became even vaguely aware of the Redwood's whisperings all around her. Their voices were urgent and fleeting, with thousands of tones tumbling over one another to form one enormous voice.

Roused suddenly from her state of complete and utter isolation, Vivian realised that no matter how hard she tried to hide from everybody what was happening to her: these desires, whatever they meant, she would never be able to conceal them from the Redwoods, for the great forest was as much a part of her as her dreadful yearnings were.

So she continued nonetheless, knowing that now, regardless, it didn't matter. The Redwoods knew her lust for suffering. She couldn't take it back, and Vivian somehow knew that, amidst everything else, it had always been there, even before she had killed the Grey.

Why should she continue to hide from it?

She saw no reason, and pressed on purposefully, closing in on Astley and Zander with every unfaltering step.

'Vivian…' A thousand overlapping tones sounded in her mind like a warning bell then, their urgency clear.

"No!" Vivian exclaimed, lifting her hands to cover her ears, though of course that made no difference, for she knew she wasn't hearing their words that way.

'You can't go on like this Vivian.' The millennia old voices of the great Redwood Forest urged her. 'This is not the path you should take. It is not in your nature. This will destroy you if you let it.'

Vivian slowed her racing pace then, dropping her arms back to hang limply by her sides, and sighed deeply.

'You're wrong.' She suddenly replied then, casting her thoughts and her words out far and wide. 'It may not be the right path for me to take, and it may well destroy me…' She told them, her inner voice fierce. 'But it is a part of me, and it will probably consume me until the end of my days.'

The emphasis she placed on that statement, even though she wasn't speaking it, was clear as day, and for a moment the Redwoods remained silent.

'Vivian…'' The countless whispering voices started, but she cut them off.

'ENOUGH!' She barked silently. 'What do you know!?'

Of course she knew she was in the wrong, but her mind was already made up on this matter, and all of the words in the world, all of the countless years of wisdom that the Redwoods had accumulated in their enormous lifetime, none of it would sway her.

'It's not just a part of my nature.' She told them then, her thoughts dripping with malice, though it was directed inwardly for some reason, rather than at the Redwoods. 'It is my nature.'

And with that final comment, stinging like razors in her heart, Vivian shut off her thoughts to the great voices all around her. It wasn't even that she ignored them, she simply didn't even acknowledge their existence, and so their words no longer bothered her, freeing her to continue her terrible hunt without distraction.

Astley and Zander, snapping at each other with frustration in their voices, had just finished checking one of their traps, having found it empty and vacant of a victim. With all the animals that had gathered at Vivian Featherstone's call last night, they couldn't believe their rotten luck.

"Astley you moron! Why did you put that trap so far off!?" Zander cursed at his partner.

"You told me to put it there!" Astley replied defensively, somehow always copping out, even when it wasn't his fault. "Don't blame me!"

The sound of a sharp smack echoed through the trees then as Zander struck his partner full on across his face. Without even a trace of guilt, the overpowering bully loomed over Astley as he cradled his throbbing cheek.

"Don't you dare speak to me like that!!" Zander hissed through gritted teeth, grabbing Astley roughly by the scruff of his clothes and dragging his face up until it was but an inch from his own. "You're a moron! If it weren't for me you wouldn't even be alive today! She would have caught you years ago!"

Of course by 'she' he meant Vivian. And again, of course, he was wrong. Astley was probably a better tracker than Zander would ever be. It was just, quite simply, that he wasn't a tyrant, and so always ended up being the one catching the sharp end of Zander's tongue, and fist too, it would seem.

A rustle amongst the bushes caught both their attentions then, and Zander dropped Astley back to the ground, drawing a small blade from beneath his loose shirt as he turned to investigate. He crept closer to the shrub that concealed Vivian, totally unaware of what lay behind, just out of sight and reach.

Astley clambered slowly and silently to his feet behind Zander, drawing a blade also from beneath his shirt, crouching low nervously.

"What the…" Zander began. But he never quite finished his sentence, as a dark silhouette lunged madly towards him.

Vivian darted from her concealment, wild rage in her eyes. Wielding a snapped off branch, she drove it forcefully into his shoulder. Zander yelled in pain and reeled backwards, but he was too slow.

She leapt onto him and dragged him down to the floor. Astley yelped with fright, turning on his heel and darted away between the trees, abandoning his sorry excuse for a companion.

Driving her heel down onto the makeshift stake she had crafted, Vivian forced several screams of agony from the evil poacher, and began to systematically pummel his face with her bare hands, not even bothering to reach for another crude weapon, she drove her fists down upon his unprotected head.

Zander jerked and jarred violently, desperately trying to struggle from Vivian's grasp, though hard as he tried, he could not escape. Her will was simply too great. But then, all of a sudden, Vivian leapt to her feet once more, and disappeared again into the shadows, not making a sound, her rage focused and deliberate.

The wounded hunter turned prey gasped for breath for a moment, shocked both by the savagery and suddenness of the attack, but then indeed also by its quick and abrupt cease. He glanced around for a moment, searching anxiously for the assailant, but Vivian was nowhere to be seen. Then he looked for his partner, Astley, but he was nowhere to be found either.

Cursing foully, Zander clutched at the stake protruding from his shoulder, weeping blood painfully. She had driven it deep, and it would take some attention to remove. He left it be, knowing she was still here somewhere, and climbed to his feet, stumbling off between the trees, his vision blurry at best.

He wobbled left and right as he scrambled forwards, dizzied from the heavy blows he had taken. The ground spun and buckled beneath his feet, though of course that was only his dazed senses playing tricks on him, and he forced his way onward.

Vivian followed easily, stalking her prey calmly, keeping perfectly hidden in the shadows. Her movements were unseen and perfect, flitting through the trees without a sound. She had let him attempt escape for a very specific reason, knowing instinctively where he would flee too.

Just as Astley had done, they were both attempting to make back for civilisation, for each of them believed that Virtus would protect them. Little did they know how wrong they were, and that neither of them would return alive.

Vivian had no intentions of sparing either of them.

Suddenly Zander was sent careering off sideways as an invisible blow struck him from the right, catching him full in the chest and stealing the air from his lungs. He gasped as he stumbled and a root protruding up from the ground caught his foot, forcing him off balance and sending him spiralling.

That had been Vivian's intention from the beginning however, and as the poacher instinctively and reflexively stretched his arm out towards the ground to catch himself, to break his fall, he only saw the small, square pressure plate, covered by leaves and dirt, at the very last second.

For that brief moment his eyes widened with horror, knowing exactly what was coming, knowing that from the very beginning she had planned this, and knowing that he had absolutely no way out.

His hand came down heavily on the small square of metal, bracing against the impact, and Zander felt the terrifying clunk of the mechanism activating beneath him.

Ripping up from beneath the ground then, just as they had done countless times upon numerous unwary and innocent animals, the hulking metal teeth crashed together with bone shattering force, trapping Zander's arm in their huge metal teeth.

The cry of sheer anguish he loosed then soared up and over the trees like an eagle carried on the strongest winds, reaching the ears of even his partner, fleeing back towards Virtus with all the speed he could muster. Astley recognised the tone of Zander's shrill cry, and a violent shudder worked its way up and down his spine, forcing him to continue onwards, driven by sheer terror.

The great jaws ripped through the puny flesh and muscle of Zander's arm, spraying blood out in every direction, and split the bone like a matchstick. He writhed and squirmed in agony, but the more he did so, the more the trap pulled on his tendons and flesh, sending fresh and amplified pain coursing through him.

Finally, Zander ceased his endless wriggling and glanced around skittishly, breathing in short and sharp bursts, the adrenaline masking the pain.

Then he saw her. The one who had attacked him. Vivian Featherstone.

He met her gaze coldly, as she stepped out from the shadows without a sound, stalking towards him over the fallen leaves, though still somehow moving silently, without so much as a crackle to accompany her steps.

"You…" He breathed, though he found sound difficult to utter, for the pain returned tenfold when he attempted to speak.

Vivian did not speak a word as she approached, tilting her head this way and that, much in the manner of the red bears, though at that moment it was the only similarity between them: the bears had never been ruled by such terrible emotion.

She had, one day long ago, sworn to live the same way, but it seemed that those promises had been long forgotten, as all too often seems to be the way.

Vivian crouched low next to Zander and he recoiled back from her in fear, though he was unable to move more than an inch or two before the awful pain forced him to remain. She reached forward and wrapped her hand firmly around the stake she'd driven into his shoulder.

With a slight smile then, one certainly born of malicious thoughts, Vivian twisted and jerked her hand, wrenching the branch painfully out from

Zander's chest. He screamed again and dropped to the floor, his eyes wide and streaming, but besides that, he could do little else.

By now the ground all around them was saturated with his blood, his face was paling noticeably, and Vivian knew if she left him there much longer, he would surely die from loss of blood. To some extent that thought pleased her, for it would be a long, slow process, but at the same time, she felt a twinge of jealousy at that notion, for she would not be the one to deliver the killing blow.

No, she had to kill him herself.

She wanted to do it herself.

Fingering the stake she had just wrenched so brutally from the poacher's chest, Vivian eyed the man dangerously. Her intention all too obvious, Zander suddenly began to writhe and squirm once more.

"No!" He gasped, forcing his words out through clenched, terrified teeth. "Don't! You can't! Please!"

But it mattered not what he said, for he certainly would not sway Vivian's decision.

She was calm now: so much so that not even her heart was racing, as it always had done in these moments in the past. Just before the kill, blinded by rage and lust, her focus had always been hazy.

Now though, everything was crystal clear, and through those new eyes, no longer blurred by such a fog, Vivian revelled in her victory even more so, her devolution very nearly complete.

Grabbing her victim by the scruff of his neck then, leaning heavily and purposefully on his wounded chest, Vivian dragged Zander down across the ground roughly, and raised her free hand high above his head, holding the bloodied stake still, her actions slow and precise.

"Please! No!" He begged again, his voice draining away to a whimper. "You can't!"

"I can." Vivian replied menacingly, her voice quiet and sure. "And I will."

And then, without even giving him another chance to protest, Vivian drove the stake down abruptly and harshly, plunging the slightly sharpened end deep into his face, twisting it and forcing it in under her weight, for it was not really all that sharp.

Zander's body convulsed and jumped horribly, but that did not stop Vivian, and she wrenched the branch out yet again, spraying herself with thick blood as she did so, and drove it in again. And again, and again, no longer in a frenzy as she had been before, but instead her movements were cold blooded and meticulous, and she savoured every detail and emotion, prolonging her kill for as long as she possibly could.

Nonetheless, all too soon it was over, and the gruesome, bloody remains that she now stood over were barely even recognisable as human.

Satisfied, adrenaline flowing freely, Vivian smiled and ambled off into the forest once more, not hesitating even once. She picked up her pace once she found the trail she was after, and then instantly she was on the hunt again, stalking the second poacher.

Astley raced through the trees still, though his pace was somewhat slowed and his breathing laboured. He had lost his way once or twice in his panic, but now here and there he saw things that he recognised: a certain shaped clearing, split trunks and broken branches, old trap sites.

He was nearly back now.

Virtus was almost in reach.

But then the hairs on the back of his neck braced and stood on end, sending a shiver crawling down his spine. He wiped the sweat away from his forehead and crouched low, glancing all around, terrified, feeling heavy eyes set upon him.

After waiting for another two or three minutes, straining his ears and eyes to the silence and the overpowering redness all around, Astley finally returned to his wary pacing, often pivoting and startling as he continued his way back to the city. Somehow he knew that he wasn't alone. He would just have to be very careful.

As it turned out however, that simply was not enough to save him. After throwing a quick look over his shoulder and seeing nothing, his breath suddenly caught in his throat, petrified.

He turned again, more slowly this time, to stare at exactly the same spot he had just examined.

Moments before, it had been empty, abandoned.

But now, after a mere second, she was there.

The Featherstone.

Vivian's eyes bore into Astley with a measured and controlled hatred that had no equal, and her stance: tall and bold, her fists clenched, reeked of a lust to hurt, to inflict pain, to torture, to kill.

The poacher swallowed hard, facing Vivian directly now, his own stance fearful and timid, just as it always had been.

"I…I'm…I'm sorry…" He stammered slowly and quietly, barely loud enough for even himself to hear, let alone Vivian. That didn't matter though. She did not need his voice to be loud in order to hear him. Had she really wanted to, she could have plucked the very thoughts from his mind.

But it wasn't his words she was interested in.

Beginning slowly, her bloodied stake still in hand, Vivian strode towards Astley with deadly purpose, closing the gap of barely thirty metres between them faster and faster. Before he knew it she was sprinting towards him, mere seconds from reaching him, and yet, amidst all that, he could not move.

Astley's feet and legs simply would not obey him. He couldn't turn away, he couldn't even blink; his gaze was fixed solely on Vivian's charging attack. Her eyes were wide and her face was full of grim satisfaction, and she even bared her teeth as she launched into the air, her features wild and animalistic.

There was silence for a second, as if the whole world had come to a standstill, and Astley's heart skipped a beat. But of course that was not the case: that was just how it felt in the heat of the moment.

Adrenaline and fear was built up so heavily in his veins, that the poacher barely even felt the pain of Vivian crashing into him at full pelt, driving her crude and improvised blade into his face. She sent him flying and cascading backwards, pinned to him fiercely, spraying the essence of his life in all directions, yet again bloodying the very place that had once been her beloved home.

17

Indeed, Astley had not been wrong. He hadn't been far from the outskirts of the great city Virtus at all. Even now as Vivian peered through the trees, wiping the blood from her eyes and spitting it from between her teeth, she could see the vague outlines of farmsteads: mills and grain houses, stores and cottages.

Knowing she couldn't return to civilisation in this state, Vivian simply abandoned her second carcass, just as she had done the first, and swept casually through the woodlands once more, heading now for Featherstone Keep.

She thought of Kael then, almost guiltily, and wondered whether he was thinking of her. If she left now he wouldn't be able to follow her, and he would remain safe. That thought comforted the young Featherstone a little.

Her calm and relaxed attitude towards the immediate abandonment of her more murderous self, frightened Vivian somewhat, as her normal human senses and emotions returned to her, flooding back in fits and flurries.

She put the thoughts out of her mind however, knowing there was nothing she could do about it now, and also that she might never even see Kael again, and simply continued northwest up towards her first home.

The rest of that day passed by in a blur, with the morning having already somehow slipped by, the hours having disappeared unseen in her calm and calculated rage. Almost before Vivian knew it, left unattended in her wanderings, the afternoon had also eluded her.

Exhausted and drained from her exertions, the young, troubled Featherstone bedded down for the night, building a fire just as she had done in the old days: the days when she and Red and Clover had been happy, and when she had not been a murderer.

Sleeping well, though dreaming in fits and starts of her terrible actions of that day, Vivian awoke to a bright and early sunrise, her fire having stifled and died at some point during the night.

When she awoke, rubbing her weary eyes, having seen far too much of late, Vivian found once again an audience surrounding her. For some reason though, as she sat up and surveyed their expectant faces, she felt as though she had let them down, and couldn't even bring herself to smile.

Had she summoned them during her sleep?

What did they want from her?

Vivian had no idea.

It was perhaps even possible that they'd followed her all day previously too, but she'd simply been too lost in thought to notice.

The Redwoods itself however, as Vivian trudged onwards, remained silent, and she thought that probably best for her, as well as for the great ancient forest, since her defiance to their words had been so outright. She doubted that she would even be able to face their voice now, and simply continued on.

Knowing she had acted rashly, now that her human logic had returned to her, Vivian thought she would regret her actions. But, strangely, she didn't. Between her lust for blood, her almost overwhelming responsibilities, and now Kael too, she had little else to live for.

Perhaps, even though all of the wrong she had committed could not be undone, Kael might give her more to live for?

Perhaps he would even forgive her?

It was an unlikely, farfetched dream, but nonetheless, we're all allowed to dream.

Finally, after far too long, Vivian reached the heavy, iron gates of Featherstone Keep, the trees thinning and the old, abandoned Keep coming into view not a moment too soon.

For the past day and night she'd heard the baying howls of her enemy in the distance, growing closer by the hour, though not showing their faces to her just yet. She knew she had very little time, and moved swiftly.

The gates creaked and squealed mechanically as Vivian nudged them open, passing through swiftly and on sure, steady feet. This was a path she had taken many times now, but each time she'd come here in the past, she'd been full of open ended questions, eager to expand her knowledge in any way she could.

Now though, clearly, things were very different. She had only one intention, and she refused to leave without the answer to her question. In fact, she doubted she would even be able to, and somehow

Vivian instinctively knew that this would be the last time she'd ever visit this place.

She still loved the ancient Keep. It was not forsaken, but by the week's end, for some reason, Vivian thought it probably might be.

In fact, her inherent knowledge that, one way or another, she may never return here, or perhaps never leave, either way, surprisingly did not fill Vivian with dread. On the contrary, it was quite a comforting thought, and indeed one that gave her a view towards a sense of completion, and perhaps even, if she was very lucky, contentedness.

It had all begun here, it seemed rather fitting that it would all end here, and that once it did, her new life would finally begin…

The enormous doors of her old home groaned on their hinges as Vivian made her way through the endless expanses of ruptured stone and charred wood that were the abandoned hallways.

As she walked onwards, for some reason her mind kicked into overdrive, throwing up memories from Vivian's past, up until that point long gone and forgotten.

Passing the now cold and dusty kitchens, the aroma of freshly baked bread and a slow roasting spit filled Vivian's nostrils, engulfing her senses completely. Of course there was no food to be had, for it was simply her memory stimulating her senses, but the sensation felt so real that she was convinced she could have entered and picked up the warm bread, just as she had done when she was a child. She remembered tearing off great chunks and savouring the taste, for there had always been something about the taste of fresh bread that she loved so.

Next, as she walked by another door to her right, beyond which Vivian remembered to be the nursery, she thought of all the days she had spent there as a young girl. Her mother and father had poured many long hours of love and affection into those early days, and Vivian knew that many more had been snatched away from her when they had been killed.

Another pang of guilt struck at her then, when the images of her most recent victims flashed before her eyes. But she waved them away, shaking her head resolutely.

They had all been bad men. She had done the world a service by disposing of them. But then of course, the Greystones had always thought the same of her family, she remembered, for they had always seen the Featherstones as evil.

Was there even such a thing as good and evil?

Vivian had used to believe there was, but now, after everything that she had endured, pain and loss, and all in fact that she had caused, suffering and anguish, the line between the two seemed blurred and faded, almost even to the point where it no longer existed.

Eventually she reached the library.

It was exactly as she'd left it, though she didn't know why she'd expected anything different. Scanning her eyes quickly over the large, rounded room, Vivian saw immediately the tome she had left open on the table, when she'd darted out in pursuit of Kael.

She smiled briefly at the thought, but then the sound of urgent bays and roars echoing in the distance reached her ears and hurried her into movement.

Pouring over the large book yet again, Vivian immediately found the passage she had last been reading.

And the greatest of all the changes came to those fearsome beasts to the south, for their power, even before William Featherstone had raised his hand, was unrivalled by any other. This new power brought to them strength and knowledge and everlasting life, never before seen in any creature.

Vivian looked up briefly as a new sound reached her ears. It was a roaring bellow: not that of the dragon she had heard the other night, though at the same time it sounded strangely familiar, hauntingly so in fact. She continued, her eyes flitting across and up and down the strange, thin columned text.

Though their power was vast, such a thing always requires a rival, for without one, there is no balance. And so, since there was no equal for these beasts, the time would come when

The Redwoods Rise and Fall

*man, just as they had created them,
would divide them, and pit one
against the other.*

*Just as before, there would be one
amongst man with the power to bring
change to the world, and restore
peace. This burden would yet again
find itself resting upon Featherstone
shoulders, for only the final heir to
William Featherstone's power,
fabled Vivian, had the will and the
strength to see it done.*

Vivian breathed deeply then, her heart racing.
She was reading about herself in the past tense now,
discovering that this task, whatever it was, fell to her,
as if she'd already completed it. Her mind was
running in circles, struggling to keep up.

She decided it was best to just push on,
knowing, or at least hoping, that it couldn't get much
more confusing.

*Her subjects would flock to her at
her beckoned call, for the wilderness
was more her home than any other
place, and true, just as it had been
for her ancestors before her, it was
under her protection.*

*In time she would discover that such
a call to the wild, such unification,
would be the only way to save them.*

Ross Turner

Though fabled by mankind beyond all measure, Vivian Featherstone's solemn promise of protection came at more cost than her subjects could ever have imagined, for many of them simply accepted her as a saviour, blind to the whole truth of the dreadful Featherstone rule.

Certainly now Vivian was struggling to understand. She read and reread the passages several times, ensuring she had not missed anything. But even then, after checking and double-checking, still it did not add up.

She could make sense of it in places, here and there, but in others, she was well and truly stumped.

Divide them?

Call to the wild?

Who would be unified?

The dreadful Featherstone rule?

The Greystone's rule had been dreadful, certainly, for the people had starved and suffered and died at their hands, much of the time most callously and carelessly.

But her mother and father's rule had never been so, or at least not as far as Vivian knew, and she had never heard anyone speak of Miranda and Dorian Featherstone otherwise.

So then, what about her own rule?

Was she so terrible?

Her people weren't suffering: as a matter of fact, they were thriving. She had given up her life to ensure their happiness and safety and security, just as she had done for the Redwoods.

Perhaps the passage wasn't referring to her people, Vivian thought then. Perhaps instead, it was referring to her. For in many ways her rule had been dreadful, but only for her, for it had come at such a great cost, and still even now seemed to do the same.

Immediately, Vivian thought of Emerson. She had known him for barely a day, if that, and yet still he had been taken from her. All she had left to give was her life, and Kael's, and if she was perfectly honest, only one of those did she care about.

She whispered a silent prayer, to someone, she didn't really know who, thankful that she had made Kael stay behind, for at least there he would be safe.

Several more hours passed and the day wore on ominously, turning to afternoon and early evening without warning. In that time, Vivian found little else of use in the library, no matter how hard she tried, or how many different books she pulled open, the answers to her many questions eluded her.

That fact seemed oddly and ironically fitting, she thought to herself with a rueful smile, as she climbed the spiralling stone staircase, leading up higher and higher into the Keep. It seemed that for her whole life the answers she had sought had escaped her, so why should things be any different now?

Naturally then, darkness followed, and Vivian made her way up to her old bedroom. Never even once since she had fled Featherstone Keep all those years ago had she returned to that room, and what she found stuck a lump of sadness in her throat.

Her old tapestries were ruined, destroyed by the fires that had raged, and here and there the walls had crumbled and rotted, though they were at least still somewhat intact, and the elements hadn't yet penetrated the room.

She hadn't eaten for some time, but Vivian wasn't hungry. In fact, she felt as though her body hadn't changed in the slightest. She wasn't any more tired. She wasn't any hungrier. She wasn't any weaker. She was simply being maintained by her vast power, ticking along, waiting for whatever was coming next.

Nonetheless though, she retired to bed, climbing in gratefully after all those long years away, though the last time she had slept here she had awoken to find that her home had been invaded.

Settling for the night, Vivian drifted off into a hectic sleep with a comforting sense of belonging and a strange smile from the past painted across her face.

Mercifully, her dreams that night were good ones.

Vivian saw Red and Clover, their every detail preserved perfectly and in pristine condition in her subconscious memory. They weren't at the forefront of her dream however, but instead quite a ways off, in the distance between the trees.

They were watching Vivian through the sea of red trunks, a pleased and content look evident on their faces. Observing from their viewpoint, they could see quite clearly that their sweet Viv was not alone.

The Redwoods Rise and Fall

The young Featherstone looked up, as if she had just awoken, and her gaze immediately settled upon Kael, staring back at her, his eyes loving and adoring, just as Red's had always been, but then somehow also in a completely different way.

There was definitely something there between them. It was something that no one could see, but at the same time, it was impossible to miss. They both felt it, and clearly Clover and Red could sense it, and they looked on approvingly, smiles spread across their furred faces, if that was even possible.

Vivian took Kael's hands then, acting on impulse, and caught him in a tender embrace. At least here in her dreams she was safe, with nothing but that moment in her thoughts: finally happy, at long, long last.

18

Somehow, though her dreams had been pleasant, more than pleasant in fact, which made a refreshing change, Vivian still awoke with a start, déjà vu prominent in her thoughts. She found herself swimming in a disgusting, sticky pool of sweat, her sheets saturated, just like the last time.

All around there was silence, besides the sound of Vivian's heavy, laboured breaths, but still she knew something wasn't right. Though she couldn't hear anything out of the ordinary, her senses told her, rather worryingly, that there was definitely something amiss.

She half expected to hear the shadow's voice creep through the darkness towards her, though of course she knew he was dead. Clover had killed him years ago, but the fear still remained in Vivian's heart, and it pounded violently as she clambered from the bed and swept across the pitch black room, her feet silent upon the cold stone.

Nudging her bedroom door open, Vivian stole away and down the corridor, as always unseen and unheard in the darkness. Even in the dim light she could see the scalded and charred walls, and she even shied away from them, fearful of the memories they brought her.

She slowly pushed open the door to her parents' old bedroom, though she didn't really know why, and checked briefly inside. For a moment she could even have sworn that she saw their figures asleep in the bed, but of course that was impossible, and it turned out to just be a trick of the shadows, playing havoc with her eyes in the night.

Sneaking back the way she had come, closing her parents' door behind her in a manner that felt strangely significant, as if that very act gave Vivian some sort of final closure that she'd been seeking for years, she strained her senses as best she could.

At first she detected nothing, and she merely wandered slowly and uneasily down the vast corridors, keeping her footsteps silent and her breaths shallow. But then, soon enough, she began to hear something, and indeed also smell something, most peculiar.

The sound was a faint, irregular clicking, echoing off the smooth stone walls and bouncing around in the darkness, throwing Vivian completely, for the reverberating noise meant she had absolutely no idea which direction it was coming from. She'd had this problem before, she remembered.

And the smell, though also bizarre, was one she did however recognise, but she could not for the life of her place it. Breathing deeply, Vivian pondered it for a minute or so, standing there alone in the darkness.

Soon enough the answer came to her, and her body turned icy cold as her realisation filled the young Featherstone with dread.

As Red would have said, it smelled like the plague: it smelled like death.

A lump caught in Vivian's throat at that memory, but at the same time, her hairs stood on end, and fear coursed through her veins like wildfire.

The odd clicking sound continued, echoing all around Vivian, but growing louder with every passing second. She had a good idea what it was now, since she'd pieced together the long-forgotten memory of the smell, though she hoped fervently that she was wrong.

Nevertheless, sure enough then, as she pressed her body firmly against the cold stone of the wall, peering cautiously round the corner at the very end of the corridor, Vivian saw the shapes she had feared, shifting through the darkness unseen, but not quite unheard. With every step the jet-black, plague ridden wolves gave themselves away, as their claws tapped and scraped lightly on the cold stone floor.

Bringing her hand up to her mouth, catching any loose sound from her breathing that would surely give her away, Vivian stole back down the corridor towards her old bedroom. She had no idea how many were in the Keep, but her heart began to race and thump heavily against her ribs once more, suspecting that it would likely be many. She darted back into her bedroom and pushed the door to, though she didn't close it all the way.

It was not the first time Greystone filth had invaded her home during the night.

At least this time she knew they were there before they knew where she was, but, in all honesty, she knew that did little to improve her chances. They likely already had her scent. She probably had only mere seconds before they were upon her.

Swallowing her fear, deciding what she needed to do, what she had returned here to do, Vivian summoned all the courage she could muster, and stepped back out into the hallway. The instant she did, she felt the atmosphere change, and the clicking stopped dead.

Within seconds, knowing she had little time to react before surely she would be killed, Vivian summoned a streaking blaze to each of her hands, launching them in opposite directions down the corridor, lighting the paths laid out before her: the paths she had chosen.

As soon as she did however, the light from the flames she conjured illuminated her enemy, almost blinding her in the process, and revealed to the young Featherstone at least a dozen wolves in each direction, poised ready to strike. The wolves too were blinded by the intense flashes of light, and were stunned for a moment.

A moment was all she needed.

Vivian took every advantage she could and moved immediately, striking out at those beasts to her right, sending them all careering off into the walls, breaking necks and spines and skulls in the process. She was more powerful than they were, and she knew it, but she wouldn't be able to put up much of a fight if she was surrounded and overwhelmed.

Sprinting between the dead bodies, the broken carcasses twitching and jerking, Vivian careered round the corner wildly. Vicious snaps and snarls were instantly at her heels, barely missing her. Vivian was spared only by the sharp turns she made, flinging herself round corners and crashing into the stone, battering and bruising her body uncaringly, for it was the only thing keeping her alive at that moment, as

the wolves skittered and skidded on the cold stone
with their sharpened claws.

Finally though, after nearly throwing herself
down a treacherous staircase, scraping and bloodying
her arm as she did so, she came face to face with yet
another dozen of the beasts yearning after her life,
blocking her way.

She launched herself into a room off to the
side of the corridor, the nearest of the wolves
snapping at her heels hungrily.

Just about managing to evade its razor sharp
teeth and bolt the door shut before it caught her,
Vivian gritted her teeth as she braced her body
against the wooden frame.

She glanced around desperately, searching for
a way out. Long ago, she remembered this room
being used for storage, and sure enough, as she sent a
brief flame skittering through the air, it illuminated
old chairs and tables and pots and pans, all coated
heavily in thick layers of dust.

The noise outside the door now was almost
deafening, howling and barking and snapping and
snarling, ramming the heavy wooden barricade
relentlessly, undoubtedly close to breaching the room.

Suddenly then, Vivian spotted another door at
the back of the room, smaller than the one she was
attempting to secure, but a door nonetheless.

Without another thought, driven by
desperation, Vivian leapt towards it, propelling
herself madly over the tables and chairs, her eyes
focused in the fading light of her flittering flame
dancing above her.

Just as she reached the door at the back of the room, ramming her shoulder against it, forcing it open, the main door behind her splintered and shattered, folding in half as the wolves barraged through it brutally. Vivian didn't stop however, shutting and locking the smaller door behind her, having to duck slightly to get through it, and turned to the room that she now found herself in: the kitchens.

She took off immediately, gathering her bearings as she ran, navigating as best she could through the vast kitchenettes, hearing behind her the sound of the second door breaking and groaning under the strain of the wolves' attacks. It wasn't long at all before they were in pursuit of her yet again, their claws scratching the floor behind her. But this time Vivian had been gifted a slight head start, enabling her to lay a trap of her own.

The first of the beasts charged through the kitchens, black as night, and blind to everything beside Vivian's scent. The others followed, vicious wolves to the hunt, but unknowingly also sheep to the slaughter.

Just before they burst into the room within which Vivian lay concealed, hidden behind a low set of counters, also covered heavily in dust, unused for years, she sprung her trap.

Exploding out in all directions, hidden in the shadows and silhouettes around the room, a hundred knives and blades erupted into action, spraying out and pouring over the attacking beasts terribly, Vivian's action brutal and unforgiving. The plagued monsters yelped and squealed and cried out in agony. Hearts were pierced and lungs were punctured in great waves as the soaring blades met their marks, over and over.

Almost in an instant, the blackened wolves fell to their demise, though some had not been killed, only wounded, the vast majority of them were not left standing. Vivian grimly rose to her feet to finish her gruesome work.

She looked upon the wolves that so desperately wanted to kill her, those that were still alive crawling and limping towards her falteringly. She sighed deeply, regret and sorrow filling her for a moment, knowing that if it were not for the Greystone's plague, these poor animals would never have had to die by her hand.

Blood trickled across the floor and stained Vivian's brown leather boots red, just as her whole life had seemed to be.

Closing her eyes, she gathered her will and focused upon the task at hand, terrible as it might have been. Vivian brought to existence yet another spark, and this one she ignited upon the jerking and whining bodies of the fallen wolves, lighting them in an instant.

Killing these poor creatures was not an act that Vivian took satisfaction in, for she loved the animals of the Redwoods so. It seemed that only the deaths of her fellow humans could satisfy her, without bringing sorrow to her heart.

Within moments the smells of singed fur and smouldering flesh and boiling blood filled Vivian nose and mouth and lungs. She gagged and wretched awfully, feeling sick to her very core at her actions, but unable to vomit, for she had not eaten a thing for quite some time now.

That, coupled with the fact that she had drawn heavily upon her power recently, both in fighting off the wolves, and in keeping herself alive and functioning, the young Featherstone was feeling decidedly weak.

Stumbling out of the smoky kitchens, smelling of scents most awful, Vivian reeled and retched as she made her way back out into the corridor: the one she had eavesdropped over Archer in all those years ago.

Gathering her thoughts, the troubled young woman leaned heavily on the wall, cold to the touch of her dirtied hands.

At least she was safe now, Vivian thought to herself.

But, sadly, that was not to last.

As the sounds of the flames died down beyond the door, the smoke filtering out beneath it, another sound snatched Vivian's attention. It was a low grumbling, a growl, like the sound Red and Emerson had always made when sensing danger.

She turned and glanced around in the darkness, unable to see a thing, but knowing instinctively, as she usually did, that something was wrong.

Just as before, she raised her hand and lighted the corridor with a small burst of flame, sending it jumping up into the air, spitting calmly with intense heat and light.

The second she did however, she almost wished she hadn't, as her sparkling ball of flames illuminated three enormous black bears. They stood unmoving, their focus entirely on her, barely six feet from where Vivian stood.

Her mouth dropped open in a mixture of awe and terror.

How had they managed to creep up on her so?

But that didn't matter then, for they closed in on her immediately, baring their massive teeth and powerful claws.

Not knowing what to do, barely even having the energy left to react, Vivian simply fled, sprinting without a sound blindly and wildly through the darkness, and the great black bears pursued her immediately, not missing a single step.

Vivian had not the energy to keep running however, for she had drained herself more than she'd realised, and within minutes her legs felt heavy like lead, and her breaths were terribly laboured. She flung herself through yet another door, locking and bolting it behind her, only to find herself trapped in a broom cupboard.

Heart racing and hands trembling, Vivian braced herself against the heavy door yet again, though this time her actions were much more desperate, and indeed also much more useless. The three massive bears took turns in throwing their enormous hulks against the thin barricade concealing Vivian.

This door was smaller and stouter than the one that had shielded her from the wolves had been, but nonetheless, the bears were more powerful, and it would stand little more punishment.

The door shook and rattled on its hinges, barely remaining within the doorframe as it bent and buckled under the huge blows. Eyes darting left and right, Vivian scanned the dim room for something she could use, somewhere she could hide.

Anything.

But it was useless.

There was nothing.

This time, it seemed, there would be no escape.

Crumpling to the floor then, sliding her back down against the shaking door, exhausted and defeated, Vivian dropped her head into her hands.

Then, for some reason, a passage from the text she'd read only the day before threw itself to the forefront of Vivian's thoughts, reciting itself in her own voice.

'Her subjects would flock to her at her beckoned call, for the wilderness was more her home than any other place…'

She hadn't understood it when she'd first read it, only yesterday, but then the fog in her mind began to lift and fade away.

'In time she would discover that such a call to the wild, such unification, would be the only way to save them.'

Perhaps, after everything that had happened, the time that the text spoke of was now: these final days of suffering.

And so, Vivian rose slowly to her feet once again, placing her hands against the barely standing door in the darkness, and purpose once again lighted her blue eyes, though they were barely lit at all after the lifelong, lingering suffering that was her world.

Vivian closed her eyes and tried to focus, doing her utmost to blot out the black bears' angry, vengeful roars as they smashed repeatedly into the door, barely still on its hinges.

She didn't have long, probably not even thirty seconds.

Focusing on the Redwoods as best she could, drowning out everything else with the silence of her own thoughts, she searched for the animals that lay hidden and concealed amidst the trees. Scanning high and low in her mind's eye, young Vivian Featherstone swept her vast gaze across the endless forests, summoning all that lay within to her aid.

Vivian had absolutely no way to know if she was having any success, and so she simply kept trying, urging on and on.

After what felt like a lifetime, the bears finally managed to break through the stout wooden door, raking through the split planks with huge claws. Able to once again see Vivian, their rage intensified, and their bellows deafened her, breaking her concentration entirely.

However, their great roars were followed by others, echoing down through the corridors, and Vivian smiled with heavy and obvious relief, as the creatures of the Redwood Forest, supposedly under her protection, came to her aid.

Red wolves and bears all charged forward, at the very front of the advance, and leapt upon the black bears that had Vivian cornered. With bared teeth and claws slashing this way and that, they began systematically ripping the three black bears to pieces.

Eager to aid her fellow creatures, Vivian burst from the storeroom, blowing what was left of the door off of its hinges, and assaulted the black bears also, her vigour and strength suddenly renewed with fresh hope. She battered them with invisible blows and great hurling streaks of fire, cutting through them with devastating effect.

Soon enough the three bears were overcome, quite easily in fact, but that was not the end of it. Terrible howls and cries echoed out in all directions then and more black wolves and bears poured into the corridor, their raging anger getting desperate now, for their ranks had been severely depleted. The odds were turning against them now that Vivian had summoned these creatures to her aid, and they knew it.

The battle raged on, with teeth and claws ripping and tearing fur and flesh in every direction.

Eventually, realising they had erred, the attacking, plague ridden monsters fled the scene, making their escape swiftly, pursued by the animals Vivian had summoned.

The wave of black charged away down the corridor, followed immediately by the surge of red, biting and snapping at their heels.

Vivian laughed weakly and collapsed to the floor, now alone, exhausted, and looking on after the creatures that had saved her life, disappearing in pursuit of the vile, blackened beasts. Relief flooded through her, and she gasped meekly, trying to regain her breath.

But then, relenting not even for a moment, in the darkness beside her, another low, throaty growl caught Vivian's attention. She snapped her head to her left, only to see an injured wolf amidst the strewn carcasses of the dead, staining the floor with red and black, eyes trained on her.

Its look was bloodthirsty, just as all the others had been. But now it had her all alone, and clearly she was spent.

Wasting no time, knowing she could at any moment turn the tables, the beast seized the element of surprise. Ignoring its injuries in its moment of triumph, the creature launched itself at the young, unprotected Featherstone.

This was it. Vivian knew she had come to the end now.

Having no time at all to react, she simply closed her eyes and sighed. All that fighting had in the end boiled down to this final moment, and at last she could accept it. She had not the strength nor the time to fight back. She simply knew and accepted that it was over.

"VIVIAN!!" A voice suddenly yelled then, and just as she opened her eyes, seeing the wolf mid-leap, mere feet from claiming her, the shadowy figure of a man collided with the great, hulking monster, catapulting into it with such force that they were both thrown madly down the corridor.

As she watched them go, shocked and mouth agape, Vivian recognised the shout, and the more she watched, as the moments turned to dreadful seconds, she recognised too the way the man moved, the way he fought, tussling with the wolf on the cold and bloodied stone.

"Kael?" She whispered softly, unable to believe what she was seeing.

But then, soon enough, disbelief turned into horror, as the fearless man's blade bit down heavily into the wolf's ribcage, piercing the demon's heart and lungs, and the monster's teeth clamped around Kael's neck, drawing blood in heavy fits and spurts.

"KAEL!!" Vivian suddenly screamed, screeching at him even as she launched to her feet and raced over to the two of them, driven on by desperation.

But by the time she got there, their efforts had both ceased, and the wolf rolled off her Kael lifelessly, the wind rushing from its gaping lungs as it crumpled into a heap on the floor.

Coughing and choking, covered in blood, Kael spluttered, and Vivian couldn't tell how much of the blood was his own, and how much was the wolf's.

"KAEL!!" She screamed again, throwing herself onto the floor beside him, not knowing what else to say or do.

Her question was soon answered however, as his wound gaped and seeped and flooded blood instantly, spraying and spreading far and wide across the cold, unforgiving stone.

She cradled him into her arms and he fell limply against her, unable to support himself.

"What the hell are you doing here!?" Vivian demanded, tears streaking down her cheeks, too shocked and too exhausted to even begin gathering her thoughts. Those were not the words she had wished to use, but in her dismay, those were the first ones that came to her lips.

But Kael didn't reply. His neck was ripped to shreds and tatters by the wolf's final attack, and he used all that remained of his strength to place his hand, cold now from loss of blood, against Vivian's cheek.

Shock and anger and denial gripped Vivian all at once, and not one of those emotions could prevail over another, leaving her simply unable to do anything other than hold Kael close.

He looked up at her tenderly for a moment, the faint glimmer of a smile touching his lips, not regretting even in the slightest his actions, for he had saved her life, and that mattered more to him than preserving his own.

Vivian clutched at his hand tightly, unwilling to let him go, but it fell weakly between her fingers.

She attempted to gather her thoughts to heal Kael's wounds, but by that point he was much too far gone, and she was so weak it would have been impossible.

Unable to speak, a heavy lump set in Vivian's throat, and her heart raced heavily in her chest. A terrible barrage of overwhelming emotions flurried through her then, coursing through her weak and feeble system, engulfing her like destructive wildfire.

By the time Kael's life slipped away, tumbling from Vivian's grasp, his hand dropping to the floor symbolically, the distraught young woman was screaming and bawling into the darkness. She did not have the time, nor the strength to save him, and her pain and her agony echoed endlessly down the blackened corridors of her old home, her suffering reverberating in every direction, hysterical for all to hear.

19

The anger and fury inside of Vivian then was both unmatched and unprecedented. The blackness all around her was engulfing, and it received the full brunt of her furious, spiteful wrath, though of course it paid no heed.

Retracing their steps back along the corridors, after having chased away the vengeful blackness that was the final intruding remnants of the Greystone's accursed plague, the animals Vivian had summoned from the depths of the Redwoods sat around her in a wide, arcing circle. Though of course they were not human, they moved very much in a manner that seemed as though they were, or at the very least that they understood the human emotion and suffering that Vivian was undergoing.

They looked upon her, at first, silently, their expressions sorrowful and understanding and comforting. But hard as they tried, it didn't matter.

Vivian simply could not cope with this any longer. Kael's body lay still in her arms, drained of all colour and now completely lifeless.

This had to be stopped forever, and it had to be stopped now, else the world would never be free from the Greystone's darkness.

"Why did you come?" Vivian asked then, her voice shaky and fragile. Her question was not aimed at one creature in particular, but rather at all of them collectively. They looked between each other for a moment, and she waited silently for an answer.

Eventually one of the red bears spoke up. His voice was deep and wise, and his muzzle tinted with grey, much like Emerson's had been, but Vivian could tell this bear had not known her family personally, but instead simply knew of them through folklore.

"Because you summoned us, Miss Featherstone." The great, shaggy bear replied, his jaw moving in a bizarre, humanlike manner as he talked, just as Red's and Clover's and Emerson's had done. "Because we are of the Redwoods. Because we are loyal to the Featherstones."

Vivian thought for a moment, coughing to clear her throat. If what the great red bear was telling her was true, then it seemed she had summoned the creatures of the forest many times, knowingly or not.

She closed her eyes then, focusing her concentration as best she could in her distraught state, still holding Kael's lifeless head in her hands. Stretching out her thoughts, Vivian searched for the elusive Redwoods all around her. It was difficult though, in part because she was in the Keep and not amongst the trees, and in part because the last time she'd spoken to them she'd been so defiant and rude, and she still felt very guilty about that.

Just as they had always been however, when Vivian eventually managed to silent her racing thoughts enough to hear their whispering voices, the Redwoods were kind and understanding, patient and forgiving: traits which they had in turn passed on to the red bears.

'I'm sorry.' Vivian formed her first words immediately, her thoughts sincere, for though in the heat of the moment her feelings always overwhelmed her so, she of course regretted what she had said.

'It is of no matter Vivian.' The hundreds upon thousands of hushed voices assured her, ringing in her mind like countless sounding bells.

'I should have listened to you…' Vivian admitted then, fear and regret welling up inside of her. But the Redwoods were not looking for further explanation or apology.

'Hush, Vivian.' They quieted her painful emotions, and instantly they were quelled. 'There is still more danger ahead. We fear deeply, Vivian Featherstone, that though your life has been fraught with peril, you have not yet reached the end.'

The question that came to Vivian's mind then was perhaps not the most rational or pressing query. It was however the one which Vivian longed for the answer to more than any, since Emerson had not been able to give it to her.

'What was the point?' Vivian asked of the Redwoods, exasperation clear even in the tone of her mind. 'Why separate Emerson from Red and Clover?'

'It had to be done, Vivian.' The Redwoods assured her. But that simple answer wasn't enough.

'No, I know that.' Vivian replied, frustrated. 'If the whole point was for something to happen so that I could kill the Greystones, then why are they still here!? I killed them all! Why didn't their plague die with them!?'

This was the question she really wanted the answer to, for Emerson had not been the one to give it to her.

Vivian knew for a fact that that responsibility lay with the Redwoods.

'It's not that simple.' The Redwoods told her then, their countless voices firm, even stern.

'I'm sure it isn't.' Vivian responded, calming and composing herself, quieting the anger from voice in her mind, but that didn't mean she was any less persistent. 'But you have to answer my question.' She insisted. 'I have to know.'

'The point, Vivian…' The Redwoods began, clearly seeing that she would not budge on this matter, though somehow their countless voices were laced with sorrow, and perhaps even guilt. 'Was to make you suffer.'

The truth in their words was not harsh, but it was undeniable, and all their age old wisdom could not take the sting from them.

Vivian was silenced. Their blunt and brutal statement took her aback, wiping her thoughts empty, leaving the young Featherstone without a clue as to how to respond.

'Wha…' She started, barely even able to form that thought, but the Redwoods cut her off, their tone crystal clear and to the point.

'You have more power than anyone else has ever been granted.' They explained. 'But that doesn't come lightly. If you couldn't control it, it would surely destroy you, for without control, it would be far too much for any one person to handle.'

'But how does that…'

'Hush, Vivian.' The Redwoods silenced her then. 'Listen. Try to understand. Your parents were taken from you. Emerson was denied his family, though you didn't know of it. Red was taken. Clover was taken. And now you have discovered Emerson's sorrow, and Kael's love, only to have those ripped away from you too…'

Vivian's heart wrenched and screamed as the Redwoods words cut and pierced her, their cruelty relentless and like nothing she'd ever heard.

"Stop…" Vivian begged, even speaking the words aloud in her torment. "Please…"

Tears coursed down her cheeks, but the Redwoods continued.

'How do you feel, Vivian?' They asked of her. 'What does your pain tell you?'

"STOP!" Vivian yelled then, jumping to her feet, abandoning Kael and covering her ears with her hands. But of course that made no difference, and the Redwoods flurrying, whispering voices did not relent.

'How do you feel Vivian!?' They urged, repeating their question harshly.

"No…" Vivian whispered, her voice shaking, barely able to control her rushing emotions behind her weakening façade.

'What do you want, Vivian!?" The Redwoods almost shouted at her then, demanding that she answer them, destroying the barrier she had hidden behind almost entirely, and finally breaking through to her.

"STOP IT!!" Vivian screamed, startling the creatures sat all around her, forcing them to flinch and back off, afraid.

'WHAT DO YOU WANT!?' The Redwoods roared silently, their false anger controlled and calculated, never without purpose.

Vivian's screeching response echoed throughout the abandoned and bloodied and tarnished Featherstone Keep, filling it all of a sudden with angry life.

"I WANT TO KILL THEM ALL!!" She exploded then, her words filled with vengeful malice and hate. "I WANT TO MAKE THEM SUFFER!!" Vivian physically shook with her outcry, the echoing sound filling her ears with her sorrowful confession.

She managed to calm herself enough to stop screaming, but it was nowhere near enough to steal the spite from her tone.

"I want to kill them all." She repeated slowly. "And then I want to die."

The Redwoods remained silent for a while then, and Vivian stood tall, her fists opening and clenching slowly, fiercely, desperately trying to restrain her raging emotions. It wasn't often she let these evil thoughts get the best of her, and usually it had only ever happened when she killed.

The lust and the vengeance always overwhelmed her in those moments, but usually she could control them.

Things were different now though.

The Redwoods had done something; Vivian didn't even know what. They had awakened something inside of her, opening it for her and for the whole world to see.

'Without that emotion, Vivian...' The Redwoods began again. 'Without that incredible composure when faced with death, your power would have overwhelmed you long ago.'

They ceased their painful words, mercifully, for a minute then, allowing Vivian a precious moment to collect what few thoughts she could muster. She did not speak however, or even form a response. She simply nodded in acknowledgement of their words, knowing, finally, that they were right, and at least that all of her suffering had not been for nothing.

The Redwoods spoke again then, their limitless voices much softer and understanding, for they had not enjoyed what they'd just had to do. But then, of course, as had always been the way, Vivian would not have been satisfied until she'd had her answer.

'It was said, most truthfully, and quite some time ago…' They began, speaking as if they were delving deep into their furthest memories. 'That satisfaction and contentment may be achieved only through dedication, perseverance and, sadly, sacrifice.'

If the great forests all around Vivian then could have sighed, they most certainly would have done, and the young Featherstone sensed somehow that her suffering wasn't the first they'd witnessed, or at least the first that they had knowledge of.

'A task such as yours requires determination, resolve, and an iron-clad will so impenetrable that it is unmatched. Sadly, young Vivian, it is the case that such things are forged only through pain and suffering, as you have unfortunately come to learn…'

Their words were laced and laden with the intricacies of bitter truth, and Vivian found that her immediate acceptance of them was almost entirely painless.

Ross Turner

'How many souls does the plague still consume?' Vivian asked the great forests then. 'Are many of our own still affected by it?' Determination replaced Vivian's despair, and her focus shifted to something that was barely even human.

'As one would expect, young Vivian...' The great Redwood Forest began, seemingly accepting Vivian's immediate and automatic transformation in an instant. 'Such a thing could only have been born from the Greystone's evil, considering their everlasting lust for power. And so, it has remained only in the creatures in the farthest and hardest to reach extents of our borders. These poor souls were the furthest from the influence of your power, and so, those of them not strong enough to resist the plague, remained still succumbed to it.'

'But it hasn't killed them?' Vivian questioned.

'Indeed not.' The Redwoods replied. 'Perhaps though, in some ways, it might have been better if it had...'

'How so?' The young Featherstone asked.

'As is the everlasting power of the forest, in many equal and opposite ways to the evil of the Greystones, some creatures were able to resist the plague, with your help.'

Vivian immediately thought of Emerson, for some reason, and somehow subconsciously knew that he was included within that group.

The many voices of the Redwoods continued.

'But others were not so fortunate, and didn't have the strength to resist it entirely. You were still only touching the very edges of your power, and thus, over such great distances, its effect waned.'

208

A lump of guilt caught in Vivian's throat, though of course she'd had no way of knowing.

The Redwoods continued.

'They were able to survive the plague, and it did not kill then, but over time it infected their bodies and their minds, and even their very thoughts.'

'And now the Greystone's evil lives on.' Vivian concluded sombrely.

The haunting and sorrowful silence that followed confirmed Vivian's suspicions, and indeed also explained to her why she had felt the Greystone's terrible lust so many times of late.

An idea began to form in Vivian's mind then. Of course, she had no way of hiding it from the vast Redwoods all around her, but equally, they had no way of stopping her, regardless of how much they might have wanted to.

Such was the extent of her power.

'How have I been summoning the creatures of the woodlands?' Vivian asked then, glancing around briefly at the creatures sat still about her as she cradled Kael's lifeless body.

'You are their saviour, Vivian.' The Redwoods replied simply. 'If you call, even if you do so subconsciously, they will come.'

'All of them?' She questioned, and again there was silence for a moment, as the Redwoods realised Vivian's intentions.

'Yes.' Came the Redwoods eventual, though admittedly wary, reply. 'Even those still diseased by the Greystone's evil are loyal to you, though they might wish to harm you, you still saved their lives…'

The hundreds upon thousands of whispering voices wavered slightly as they gave Vivian the explanation she desired, for they could sense exactly what she planned to do with it, and knew she would not be swayed from her decision.

And so, with that, perhaps the most important and momentous decision of her life, finally made, Vivian stretched out her vast thoughts and touched the very corners of the Redwoods Empire. She found the task easy, though clearly it was something she'd been unable to do all those years ago, when she'd believed that she had first vanquished the Greystones' evil. Over time her power had grown and developed, and now, it seemed, there was nothing that could stop it.

The early morning sun peeked its head cautiously over the horizon, streaming light across the tips of the great Redwood ocean. Jutting up amongst the vast landscape, stained black and grey against the red all about it, Featherstone Keep protruded dangerously into the brightening sky.

Vivian saw everything in that moment: all of the creatures and animals around her, in every direction to the furthest and most distant reaches of her vast empire. She encompassed them all simultaneously, both those free from the plague, and those bound by it. Regardless though, they all longed for her help, for her protection, for her to save them.

But the young Featherstone knew, just as the people of Virtus had wished she would save them, that she couldn't.

It simply wasn't possible.

As much as they might have believed that she had done, it wasn't the case.

They had saved themselves.

She was the virtus of the People - The People's Power - supposedly. But Vivian knew now, amongst every else, that she had only ever provided direction. She may have set things in motion, but she was a figurehead, a symbol, a light amidst the darkness.

They hadn't needed a saviour. They had simply needed guidance. They had built their own lives back up from the dust, not her.

So now, not only faced with the duty of once again removing the Greystone threat, but also cleansing the whole of the vast Redwood Forest, right to its farthest reaches, Vivian somehow realised that, in fact, this task was no different.

Virtus was now thriving and, seemingly, totally self-sufficient without her. She wasn't required any more, now that she had re-established the House. If she could save the Redwoods, she knew the same thing would happen, and after the initial shock of it all, she would again no longer be needed. She could finally be free.

She had saved Virtus, or rather set things in motion, by killing the Greystones. And now here, somehow, for some reason, their plague still resided in the souls of these poor creatures.

As much as Vivian didn't want to take their lives, she had done plenty of things in the past that she hadn't wanted to, and certainly hadn't enjoyed. She had endured too many dreadful pains that no one should have to go through.

She would just have to grin and bear it, one last time. It had to be done. She had to rid the world of this evil once and for all, no matter the cost.

She had to balance the scales, for, in reality, that was all that was being asked of her.

That was all that had ever been asked of her.

The young Featherstone turned her attention back to the creatures she could sense all around her then, all the way through the vast Redwoods, their senses all turned towards Featherstone Keep, eagerly awaiting their summons. The difference between them in her mind now was so obvious: those that were infected and those that weren't, and even from so far away as they were, she could still feel them longing to kill her.

"Come and claim me then" She taunted them then, her thoughts thrown with such authority that they instantly became a command.

And so, in that single instant, Vivian called to her old home, the great Featherstone Keep, every creature from the entire Redwood Empire, both good and evil, cleansed and infected alike. They all descended upon her like great crashing waves, oblivious to the mayhem that was about to ensue.

Whatever the outcome, today, this would be settled, once and for all.

20

Vivian heard them first, as did the bears and wolves still sat about her. Their ears pricked up and their eyes widened with the realisation at what Vivian had just done, for they of course couldn't sense her thoughts in the way the Redwoods could.

The screeching and bellowing roars that ripped through the trees and across the sky in that moment were deafening, and instilled with the chilling knowledge of battle just on the horizon.

"Get down to the gates!" Vivian ordered those creatures sat around her still, and they immediately obeyed, charging down the corridor in an instant, responding to the roars echoing down the vast hallways just as much as they did to Vivian's instruction.

For a blissful moment then Vivian found herself alone, and once again cradled Kael's now cold carcass. Wiping tears from her eyes, she laid him to rest upon the cold, hard stone, peeling her hands from his clothes and skin, sticky with blood.

She wanted to say goodbye somehow, but she couldn't bring herself to even kiss his forehead.

It was too late.

Her Kael was gone now.

With tears standing in her eyes, Vivian turned her back on him and tore down the corridor, careering round a corner at the end and charging up the winding spiral staircase.

She climbed and climbed, her legs burning from the exertion, but she did not stop. Soon her chest was heaving and she was so short on breath she was practically wheezing, but still she did not relent. It was as if she was punishing herself for something, for many things, which were simply out of her control.

Finally, after what felt like yet another lifetime, Vivian burst through the door to the room that had always been hers.

From her perch in the smallest window of the highest tower of her home, Vivian threw her gaze across the stony mountains in the far distance to the south, lighted gold and yellow and orange, and somehow even purple and blue in the morning sunlight.

And just as she did, her eyes coming to rest upon those great peaks so far away, the black dragon exploded from the horizon, bellowing its ear splitting screech as it did so, its massive form majestic and dreadful against the glorious back dropped skies.

From her window too Vivian could see the sea of trees all around her shaking and succumbing as all manner of creatures poured towards the Keep, responding to her summons, looking up to her with a mixture of longing and desperation.

Then, amidst the flurries of red and brown coats swarming below her. Vivian could also see dots of black darting between the trees as wolves and bears and even some unnamed creatures pursued her.

And so the battle began.

The second those beasts burst from the undergrowth and onto the killing grounds that were the lands surrounding Featherstone Keep, blood began to flow.

The sight that beheld Vivian then was a gruesome one, as animals of all shapes and sizes crashed into each other, ripping flesh and muscle from bones and tendons, tossing them away, and then charging again, spraying blood and bile and other such substances in all directions.

At first it seemed that the fields below her were simply dotted with black shapes, but soon enough more and more began to pour from the shadows of the trees, and the piles of dead began to rise high.

Unable to look upon the devastation any longer without intervening, for it was entirely her doing, Vivian's body began to move. Her muscles acted even without her permission, and her limbs manoeuvred the young Featherstone up on the ledge of the window she was observing from. She squeezed through the narrow gap without a second thought, even as if her actions were preordained.

She paused for a second and glanced up, seeing the horrendous black dragon hurtling towards her through the brightening morning sky, its gaze fixed solely on her.

And then she jumped.

Vivian leapt from her perch, sailing out away from the tower, weightless for a single, magnificent moment, but for a moment only, before she plummeted to the ground like a rock, faster and faster, gaining terrifying speed.

Within seconds the earth was upon her, and her feet smashed into the ground with a crack like thunder. Beneath Vivian's weight and tremendous force the very ground shook, turning every head in her direction. But she did not wait to judge their responses, and instead leapt straight into action.

Clawing through the air with all the speed she could muster, Vivian hurtled towards an enormous black bear immediately to her left, smashing into the brute's chest before it had time to react. With a satisfying crack the beast reeled backwards and bellowed in pain. But that wasn't enough for young Vivian, and her attack signalled the battles around her to reignite, as she launched herself onto the bear and pummelled its face with her bare hands. Instilled with the strength of her vast power, delivering dreadful blows, she crushed the brute's skull into oblivion.

The bear reminded Vivian briefly of Clover, when she had been infected by the plague, but that memory didn't last long, as she poured every ounce of her efforts into reigniting the battle she had already started.

Suddenly then, her actions lighted by the rising, early morning sun, Vivian whipped her gaze round, sensing she was in danger. And sure enough, just as she was swept into darkness, the sunlight illuminating her blotted out by great, black wings, the terrible dragon was upon her.

The great serpent bore down towards her with its monstrous talons outstretched, cascading towards the ground with tremendous speed.

It was all Vivian could do to avoid the monster's grasp as she dove desperately to the side, barely scraping her escape. She landed heavily and winded herself, but that didn't matter.

The great, black dragon screeched in anger and frustration as its claws sunk into earth and carcasses with heavy thuds and rips. It's momentum carried it forwards a few paces before a single beat of its vast wings lifted it off into the sky again, snatching two of Vivian's own as it did so.

The two enormous bears were plucked from the ground with ease, as if they were entirely weightless, and the dragon carried them off into the sky for a minute or so, blood dripping from its talons, before dropping them from a terrible height.

Vivian couldn't watch as they crashed down through the canopy of the forest, plummeting towards certain death, and the dragon's brutal and seemingly callous actions only strengthening her resolve further.

The battle continued to rage on.

Again, and again, and again, the evil and lust filled dragon dove down to claim Vivian, and time and time again she evaded its attacks, only frustrating the beast evermore. With each strike, images of Emerson flashed through Vivian's mind, as she saw others being carried off and killed, just as he had been. But she pushed those thoughts from her mind as best she could, and focused on the task at hand.

Vivian struck down another creature, this time a large, black wolf, as it launched itself at her with bloodlust in its wide eyes, and a familiar surge of guilt filled her heart, though of course she had no choice but to continue.

Then the skies darkened once more and she crouched low, preparing for yet another attack from above. But this time the strike came slower, and something felt different. Vivian looked up. The dragon was slowing its descent, flapping its huge wings to keep its massive body aloft.

Something was different.

Something was wrong.

The beast took in a great, rumbling breath, inhaling deeply and puffing out its chest. Its black eyes locked onto Vivian's with terrible menace, and in that moment, though there was nothing she could do about it, she realised what was coming.

Her whole body tensed rigidly, and fear gripped her in its unescapable vice.

Many fairy tales and legends of old had spoken of winged serpents that could turn you to stone in a single glance, that could fell a hundred trees by simply beating their wings, and that could breathe vast columns of fire to incinerate their foes. None of the stories however, no matter how embellished they might have been, through years of telling and retelling, came even remotely close to describing the devastation that followed then.

When the monster exhaled, lurching its great head forwards as it did so, out of its mouth churned great billows of vile, black miasma, rushing and expanding into swelling clouds.

Vivian looked on in dismay, as did her fellow creatures fighting all around her, as the plague descended down relentlessly upon them.

It engulfed them completely, spreading out in every direction as it smashed silently into the ground, racing off all around.

There was nowhere to run. It was impossible to hide, for the plague was everywhere. And when it touched her skin, when she breathed it in, when it claimed her, Vivian felt instantly overwhelmed by it. The pain was worse than she ever remembered; even from the first time she'd felt it when she'd tried to save Clover.

The plague burned at her eyes and her skin, and when she breathed it in, gagging desperately for fresh air, it attacked her lungs and her heart.

For a moment there was nothing but the feeling of death. Vivian had experienced that before, several times over, but this feeling was altogether new, and infinitely more painful. She felt as though her lungs were aflame as the black miasma attacked her, robbing the young Featherstone of her senses, and of all feeling besides agony.

As hard as Vivian tried to focus her thoughts, it was simply too difficult, and she quickly began to feel death closing in on her, crushing her life from the inside out. Her burning lungs ached for fresh breath, and her eyes had sealed tightly shut now, and her body screamed for relief.

Finally, after what felt like an eternity without respite, Vivian managed to form the remnants of a focused thought, stringing glimpses of them together to form a single, coherent command. And with that, with as much power as she could muster, she forced the plague from her body, expelling it from her lungs and from her blood, and even from her mind, where it had begun to worm its malicious way into her thoughts.

She screamed as the pain ebbed away, bit by bit, before it eventually vanished entirely. She took a deep, free breath of fresh air, filling her lungs, and opened her eyes, squinting against the light, now that the black fog had lifted.

But she immediately wished she hadn't.

Strewn all about young Vivian, in every direction that she could see, right the way up to the treeline, were the bodies of her fellow fallen creatures. Not a single one of them had survived the attack. Many of them still twitched and convulsed, for the death that the plague brought was not a quick and kind one, but instead a long, slow and torturous one.

Silence hung all around like death.

Her immediate and instinctive response was to run to the aid of those still clinging to life, but she was not given the chance. The great black dragon still circled above, and those animals already infected by the plague, black wolves and bears, unaffected by the miasma, for it was already a part of them, stalked towards her through the littered carcasses.

Vivian took a faltering step back.

There wasn't time to help the others.

The Greystones were closing in on their prize.

But before she had chance to make a decision, a deep, rumbling voice echoed all around, shattering the silence.

"Kill her!" The dragon's dreadful voice resounded, booming over the battlefield.

And with that command, the dozen or so enormous black bears and wolves that were carefully fanning out around Vivian, stalking her, leapt into action, surging forwards, churning dead bodies behind them in their wake.

Teeth and claws lashed out at her, and it was all Vivian could do to evade them and avoid being ripped to pieces. She knocked some aside at the last moment, sending the maddened creatures flying with invisible blows, and others she simply had to dive out of the way of.

She was drastically outnumbered however, and it was only a matter of time before her defences began to slip.

First came the claws across her lower back, scraping four long, horizontal tears that cut easily through her loose clothes and paper thin skin, knocking harshly against her spine as they crossed it.

Next came the blow to her head, as Vivian spun and reeled away from the bear that had sliced her back, the same creature lunged forwards with unimaginable speed for such a bulky brute, and delivered a crushing blow down upon Vivian's unprotected forehead. The strike sent her lurching backwards and she immediately lost her footing, sprawling out onto the ground unceremoniously.

That was their cue.

Immediately they were upon her. Like hungry vultures, the attacking hordes swarmed in upon the vulnerable Featherstone, and her long overdue mauling at last began.

The first to her was one of the black wolves. It clamped its jaws down upon Vivian's leg in a vice grip, ripping and tearing at muscle and grinding and grating at bone with all its might. The next beast reached her and bore down upon Vivian's flailing arm, doing its best to reduce it to shreds in seconds. And finally, before Vivian finally managed to gather her senses, a bear locked its enormous jaws around her shoulder and collarbone, immobilising her completely.

She screamed desperately and writhed this way and that, but she could not break free, no matter how hard she struggled. The pain soon became too much to bear and it overwhelmed her senses.

With one final fight, with all the strength she could summon, Vivian snatched at her will and struck out at the dozens of creatures swarming down upon her, as she lay on the cold ground.

Her power was still such that she sent them all reeling and flying backwards, knocking them from their feet and dazing them, just long enough to make her escape.

Though her body was aflame with fresh agony, and her limbs and chest oozed and coursed with thick, red blood, Vivian launched to her feet and took off as fast as she could, barely able to support her weight on her leg, even with the help of her powers to mask the pain and keep the limb together.

Once again she headed for the comparable safety of the Keep, though she doubted it would protect her for long.

Within seconds, though barely quickly enough, she made it inside, almost throwing herself through the doorway and silently ordering it forced shut behind her. The heavy doors obeyed her command immediately and swung heavily on their hinges, slamming closed with a resounding bang that echoed past Vivian and off down the many corridors beyond her.

Breathing fast and gasping for relief, Vivian crumpled to the ground, unable to take her own weight on her ruined leg any longer.

Gritting her teeth, sweat pouring from her, Vivian pulled her focus in as best she could, and attempted to sew together her injuries, for if left untreated, they would very soon turn grave. Though she doubted her luck would hold out long enough for her to die of her injuries.

She knew she had very little time, for the doors would not hold up forever, and even through her narrowed focus, directed intently upon the task of healing, she heard the black dragon's terrible, bellowing shriek, and the final, dreadful assault upon Featherstone Keep began.

21

Though it took Vivian barely even two minutes to roughly patch back together her leg and arm and shoulder, that was all it took for the plague ridden army chasing her to reduce the heavy wooden barricade to splinters, and all too soon they poured into the Keep.

Vivian however, was ready for them, and had already gathered her strength to strike.

The great, black, hulking forms of the wolves and bears were framed against the lighted backdrop of the morning sky as they entered the Keep, and it was in that narrow funnel that Vivian focused her attack.

Great searing flames and heavy, invisible blows rained down upon her attackers, and those that were not taken victim by her vicious strike, soon retreated back to safety. Vivian screeched angrily as she directed more and more of her will into the assault, and her victims screamed in pain equally.

Finally, her strength severely sapped, Vivian relented, and saw with satisfaction that the doorway was clear once again, save the charred carcasses that remained smouldering and unmoving.

Breathing a heavy sigh of relief, collapsing to the floor again, drained of her strength, Vivian smiled briefly at her small success.

Victory was short lived however, for within moments the light that illuminated the doorway darkened, blocked out by something, and Vivian felt a familiar and daunting rush of air surge through the entrance and down the hallway towards her.

Without warning then, without so much as a sound, the powerful black dragon ripped through the archway and launched itself towards Vivian, tearing up the stone floor with its massive claws and crushing the doorway with its huge shoulders.

It snapped and lurched at her hungrily, desperately, all the while its dead, black eyes locked on hers. Mercifully for Vivian though, the age old stonework held firm, and though the walls cracked and split, they did not crumble.

"You won't escape!" The dragon's dreadful voice sounded, echoing deeply all around the young Featherstone. "Not this time!!"

The monster shrieked deafeningly then and took in a deep breath.

But Vivian knew exactly what that meant, and without a second thought turned and fled for all she was worth, praying that the stones would hold firm and that the dragon's plague ridden miasma would not catch her.

Though it made no sound, she knew it was pursuing her, and though the dragon's echoing cries faded slightly behind her, she knew also that the beast would not relent.

The beast bellowed and screeched in frustration as Vivian disappeared down the winding corridors, and withdrew its serpent-like head from the doorway. Taking to the skies, it proceeded to circle the Keep, training its eyes for any sign of its prey.

Pausing for a moment, pressed firmly into the darkest corner she could find, Vivian allowed herself a few terrified and shaky breaths, though she did not dare move.

She could hear the dragon's powerful wing beats, even from beyond the thick walls of the Keep, and could sense that the monster was encircling her, waiting for her to reappear. Knowing she couldn't stay here for long, for others would surely soon be sent in to flush her out, Vivian rose unsteadily to her feet and kept moving.

Her body was in tatters: she limped heavily on her ruined leg and clutched at her shredded arm, though it no longer bled so profusely.

She had no choice but to go on.

Regardless of the fact that it probably made very little difference, Vivian crouched low and kept her back to the wall as she moved. Where she was heading she didn't really know, for as soon as the dragon saw her, no matter where she was, she knew it would be upon her in a heartbeat.

She came to a corridor then that skirted around the kitchens on the ground floor, and such, because it ran round the whole of the kitchens, it was lined with windows that looked out over the Keep's ground.

Vivian's heart was in her mouth.

The beginnings of an idea began to form in her mind, and she realised that even subconsciously she was making her way towards the Keep's main dining hall. This corridor, however, stood between her and her destination.

Taking a deep breath and dropping to her hands and knees, gritting her teeth against the pain, Vivian began to crawl forward, trying desperately to keep out of the light that streamed in through the dirtied windows. Every few seconds a shadow darted past and blocked the light that shone in, even if just for a moment, for the great dragon still circled the Keep endlessly.

A terrible bellow echoed out then, reaching Vivian's ears and shaking the panes of glass above her in their frames. Waiting for the shadow to pass by again, she stole a quick peek out through the filthy glass, barely able to see anyway. It was enough however, and with a mixture of grim satisfaction and resolute need, Vivian noted that her previous summons had certainly not been ignored.

Hundreds of creatures poured from the forests all around now, charging towards the Keep and the black beasts guarding it, fighting to defend their homes. They were, in essence, the life and blood of the great Redwood Forest, and without them, it would have been nothing but an empty shell.

Vivian smiled to herself, pride surging through her body, renewing her.

She lingered a moment too long however, savouring that feeling, and, as is usually the way with human emotion, it was a costly mistake.

Spying her immediately as it made its pass, patience winning out over emotion, as again is usually always the way, the monstrous black dragon shrieked in terrible exultation and tucked its wings in close to the sides of its hulking body. It adopted an unstoppable dive and plummeted down towards its prey without the slightest hint of yielding.

Vivian screamed a foul curse and took to her feet sprinting, her concealment blown by her own stupidity. Her feet skidded on the cold stone floor as she launched herself forward, flashing past the windows, time seeming to slow to a crawl as the hulking black dragon loomed closer with every fleeting glance.

Eventually, just before she cleared the corridor, she ran out of time, and the beast careered into the side of the Keep, smashing straight through the glass and stone and wooden timbers effortlessly.

Shards and splinters of rock and wood and glass exploded out in every direction and the monster shrieked as it ploughed through the lot of them, snapping and clawing at its prey with all its might.

Vivian was thrown forwards by the impact of the collision, and screamed in fresh pain as chips of stone and timber and shards of glass embedded themselves into her back, running up and down the full length of her spine. Clattering to the floor, her head knocking viciously against the stone, Vivian rolled onto her side and looked back at the beast that was so desperately pursuing her, trying to focus on it with dazed vision.

The dragon struggled and writhed and yearned out towards her, and she just lay there watching it, only infuriating the beast further. But the corridors were too narrow, the walls too well built, and the stones too set in time to be knocked aside so easily.

Infuriated, the dragon withdrew, fixing Vivian still with the same steely gaze, and took once more to its circling watch.

The fabled Featherstone simply lay there for a few moments longer, her head spinning and her thoughts vague.

Finally, as the throbbing in her head began to subside, and as her mind began to clear, Vivian dragged herself reluctantly to her feet. Every bone and muscle and joint in her body ached and throbbed, and she doubted they would be able to withstand too much more punishment.

Nonetheless, she pressed on, driven solely by the fact that the longer it took her to face the plague ridden beast, the more innocent creatures would die. That thought might have done little to lessen her pain, but it definitely spurred her on, and she lurched forward awkwardly, sharp shots and streaks of pain dancing up and down her back and legs and arms as she moved.

Eventually, staggering down several more dimly lit corridors and round a final bend, Vivian threw herself against the heavy wooden door that she knew led to the Keep's main dining hall. And sure enough, as she forced the door open on its squealing hinges, it was beneath the high ceiling of the dining hall that she stumbled, dropping to her knees on the hard, unforgiving floor.

The room was enormous, lined with long, dusty tables, each with a hundred and more chairs placed around it. The walls, where they were not magnificent stained glass, were hung with embroidered tapestries that depicted scenes from folklore, one of which, quite ironically, even portrayed a dragon encircling the Keep.

The haunting and now familiar black shadow swept across the stained light cast in through the windows, and Vivian knew she had but seconds before the beast knew she was in here. She hoped, in her desperation, that if the beast tried to enter here, she could funnel what remained of her strength to kill it. It was, after all, the only room in the entire Keep big enough to hold, and hopefully trap the great dragon.

It was a plan likely flawed beyond belief, but it was her only plan, and thus Vivian had little choice.

Sure enough, as if on cue, the looming shadow swept closer, blocking out almost all the light that filtered in to the great hall.

The ceiling itself was a mixture of stone and wooden timbers and slate, and Vivian knew it wouldn't take very much time at all for the dragon to break through and reach her.

Within seconds then, rumbling and shaking beneath the beast's weight, the ceiling began to split and splinter and cave in as the dragon came to perch atop the roof. Ripping down with its massive claws, the beast tunnelled its way easily through, directly above Vivian.

Sprinting again now, heading for the opposite side of the hall so that the monster did not come down directly on top of her, it was all Vivian could do to avoid the falling debris: timbers, stone blocks and heavy clumps of falling slate. More than a few times she was even forced to cast heavier chunks aside using her waning power to save herself being crushed and killed.

The beast made short work of the stone and timbers protecting the fabled Featherstone, and even as they still rained down upon her, the serpent-like creature dropped into the dining hall with an earth shattering crack, like a thunderous drumbeat, shaking the very foundations of Vivian's old home.

Its massive bulk buckled and crushed and destroyed the long rows of tables and chairs, shattering them without a thought and churning the room to ruin even as it entered.

Turning to face the monster, looming over her hungrily and with an all too obvious delight, Vivian thought that its features were almost even demonic as it grinned at her evilly. She examined the black, plague infected dragon properly for the first time, now so close she could feel the beast's hot, steaming breath, ridden with the reek of the plague: with the stench of death, as Red would have said.

Its scales glimmered black and bloodied in the sunlight that streamed in through the crevasse it had opened in the roof above, and its black eyes flashed hungrily and longingly.

Finally, seemingly unable to wait any longer, the dragon reared its monstrous head and let out an ear splitting shriek, deafening Vivian and reducing her to her knees, head bent down, overpowered completely.

"YOU'RE MINE!"

22

The dragon closed in on the unprotected Vivian, helpless now in the looming shadow of the hulking monster. She had thought she'd be able to fight it, but she was too tired and too weak. It was as if the beast's very aura robbed her of her strength, and she even felt the plague seeping out from it, contaminating the very air she breathed.

Eyes flashing and head rearing triumphantly, the dragon savoured its victory, grinning as it towered over its feeble prey.

But then its eyes flashed no more, and the shimmering of its steely black scales ceased, as the light streaming in from the shattered windows and the gaping hole in the roof above was blocked. An eerie darkness fell over the vast dining hall, and they seemed frozen in that instant.

Hesitating for a moment, an unsettled and concerned look crossed the triumphant dragon's scaly face. The beast's eyes still bore into Vivian's, though their harshness faltered slightly, tainted by doubt, and even fear. Vivian held the dragon's gaze however, resolute as always, though she clutched her many wounds tenderly, as the colour continued to drain from her face.

For a second there was nothing but silence, and a strange apprehension hung in the air between predator and prey, as if something greater than either of them was taking place, that neither of them had any idea about.

The pool of blood forming about Vivian was growing visibly, almost by the second, and she could feel the steady drain on her power and her strength increasing gradually in turn.

Suddenly then, after a few more seconds of eerie quiet, the silence was shattered by yet another ear splitting shriek; it was a roar so loud and so powerful that it shook the very ground and foundations beneath Vivian's feet.

Even though the terrific bellow felt as if it rattled Vivian from the inside out, the sound was much deeper, and for some reason sounded as though it was much more ancient, with many more years of experience behind it, than that of the black dragon looming over her.

Then, without warning, a colossal set of talons extending from legs wrapped in enormous red scales reached down through the crevasse the black dragon had created. The claws immediately found their mark, and wrapped firmly around the beast cornering young Vivian.

The black dragon shrieked and writhed in panic, but it stood not even the slightest of chances. One clawed foot wrapped around its torso, puncturing its ribs and spraying out thick, hot blood in every direction, drenching Vivian in the process. And the other, at the same time, wrapped around the beast's great serpent-like neck, threatening to crush the life from it in an instant.

Its size and strength obviously paling in comparison to the colossal creature now restraining it, the black dragon struggled desperately as it was slowly dragged up from the floor. Huge rushing winds gushed in through the ravine in the ceiling as the creature above flapped its enormous wings, and dragged Vivian's attacker out the way it had come.

In its panic, blinded by fear, the black dragon lashed out at Vivian with its long, flicking tail, knocking her feeble frame aside with ease, sending her sprawling painfully to the ground.

Weak and dizzied and dazed, she didn't have chance to prevent or evade what happened next.

In a final desperate attempt to seize its prize, the black dragon lunged forwards, beating its wings for momentum with a cry of pain as the claws around its body sunk yet even deeper. But its efforts weren't wasted, and it wrapped its talons around the wounded Vivian, scooping her up from the ground and slicing its claws into her as it did so, drawing fresh blood and prompting a terrified scream.

The sounds of her cries reached the scaly ears of the great red dragon above: the beast that had come to her aid.

Upon hearing her distressed screams the red dragon's heart quickened, and he feared for Vivian's life, having of course no way of knowing that the black dragon had her within its talons.

A powerful beat of his wings sent him soaring upwards, dragging the black dragon flailing along up with him, and in turn also dragging Vivian up and out of Featherstone Keep, and high away into the now midday sky.

Vivian slipped in and out of consciousness, losing torrents of blood now, the thick droplets coursed down her arms and legs and trickled between her fingers, before dropping away below her and cascading down towards the ground so far away, lost amidst the red ocean of treetops below them.

Her stomach churned and Vivian caught brief, fleeting images of Featherstone Keep and the battle still raging within its grounds, as she was whirled and spun through the thin, cold air.

Thankfully though, even in the brief glimpses and glances that she did manage to catch, it seemed that her plan had worked, and the united might of the Redwoods and all of its inhabitants had overwhelmed the darkness and evil of the Greystone plague. Only a bare few still remained, for it seemed that eventually, against all odds, with the right guidance and direction, good had at last won out over evil.

One that did still remain however, barely clinging to life, still clutched the young Featherstone in its grasp.

Even now though, she could feel the great black dragon's grip on her loosening, as death hurried to claim it. Its great claws sliced through her body, like a hot knife through butter, scratching and raking at her bones and her insides, spurting fresh blood and new pain with every passing second. Until finally, after what felt like a lifetime, there was no more blood to be had, and no more pain to be felt.

The more its grip loosened, the further she sunk through its claws, and the deeper they cut through her, slicing her open with ease.

Craning her head and twisting urgently this way and that, Vivian tried desperately to look up and get the red dragon's attention.

But it was of no use.

The great red monster that had rescued her finally drained the life from the plague infected black dragon: its wounds far too great to carry on.

Then it happened.

The beast's head dropped, the last of the Greystone's evil finally falling beneath the combined might of the Redwoods, and, in turn, its grip failed completely.

There was a brief second of fresh pain again as the tips of the monster's claws caught on Vivian's ribs, and then she was free falling, plummeting down towards the ground, with nothing between her and certain death, far, far below.

Those moments, seconds, minutes, however long Vivian fell for, she had no idea, passed by in a blur. Her eyes flitted open and closed as she passed in and out of consciousness, catching brief glimpses of the deep blue sky and the vast seas of red, and even occasionally her Keep.

Flailing wildly, she couldn't feel her arms or her legs as she spun and tumbled and plummeted, either through shock or loss of blood, or both.

Eventually, midway through her fall, Vivian passed out completely, her body beaten and battered, and simply unable to take any more punishment.

Everything went black.

She didn't see the colossal red dragon drop his prize and tuck himself into a plummeting dive, dashing desperately after Vivian, panic in his eyes as their saviour plummeted to her death.

23

When Vivian awoke, her first thought was that surely she was dead, for there was not a sound to be heard all around.

She had dropped from the black dragon's grasp, passed out, hit the ground, and died.

That would undoubtedly have been the most simple, and indeed easiest option: to never have to wake up again.

The thought was blissful.

Unable to move, or even muster the strength to open her eyes, Vivian just lay there and listened.

Nothing. Not a sound, not even a breath to be heard.

Surely this must be it. She was dead. It was all over.

But it was not to be.

Yet again, somehow, she had cheated certain death, even though, not for the first time, she had welcomed it so freely, and with such open arms.

Finally cracking her eyes open, mustering all the strength she could find, she saw the sky above was dark, a very deep and rich blue, dotted with a million stars. It was as if someone had laid out a sheet of rich velvet and stretched it across the great expanses above her, spatting it with glitter in the process.

The moonlit and endless dark of night had finally descended upon her, only this time it would stay with her forever.

All around her sat the animals of the forest that she had summoned to battle: to defend their homes. They were silent, blood stained, and some badly injured from the struggle. Nonetheless though, they watched and waited patiently, all eyes on their saviour.

Amongst those creatures, naturally, was the colossal red dragon that had saved Vivian's life, or at least attempted to with every fibre of its being.

The beast was much larger than the black dragon had been, with a longer neck and snout, flushed red scales, thick forearms, and very broad shoulders.

Folded onto its back were its enormous wings, which clearly had seen much use, and were ripped and torn in places.

Even from that single glance, Vivian could somehow tell that this creature was much older and more powerful than the black dragon had been; regardless of its size, this was a monster that had seen many, many moons, and clearly more than a few of those moons had been stained red.

"Vivian…" The colossal beast spoke then, uttering that single word as if countless years, decades and millennia had all hung upon it.

His voice was ancient, but not worn, instead embedded with a great and grave wisdom, gained only through endless difficulty and acceptance.

The dragon's scaly lips and mouth moved in a way that seemed impossible, forming each syllable and sound with its reptilian snout in a manner that was most unnerving, much like the great red bears had always done. Hot upon Vivian's cold, drained body, the beast's breath warmed her to her very core.

Renewed somewhat simply by the sound of his voice, Vivian forced her useless limbs into action, dragging her heavy, ruined body to sit up, propping her weight as best she could on her wounded arms, turning to face the dragon directly.

"Are they all dead?" Vivian asked first, though the words were heavy in her heart and she grimaced at the sound, and even as she heard them leave her lips they stung at her. She had never wanted to harm anything of the mysterious Redwood Forest, but sadly she had been left no choice.

It had been the only way to save the woodlands.

Victory, it seems, like sacrifice, even if meant for good, is always double-edged, and often causes the most pain.

"Yes, Vivian." The great dragon replied, speaking softly in his rich, deep voice, sensing her torment and anguish. "I'm afraid so."

Vivian looked at the colossal beast inquisitively then, seeing that what he had just done pained him just as much as it did her, if not even more.

"What's your name?" She asked of him then, and the great dragon locked his eyes onto her for a moment, taking a deep breath, instinctively knowing what her next question would be, and bracing himself for the harsh truth he would have to deliver.

"Orion." He replied simply. "My name is Orion."

"And what about the bla…" Vivian began, but Orion cut her off before she had time to finish.

"Euan." He said, his voice brimming uncontrollably with sorrow. "His name was Euan. He was my son."

Hit then by a vast, fresh surge of guilt, Vivian's breath was stolen from her, and her body seemed to seize, locking her within her own torment. It may not have been directly her fault, for she hadn't created the plague in the first place, but it certainly had been her doing that had pitted father against son.

How many innocent families had she ripped apart?

She dared not imagine.

The thought was unbearable.

A mournful silence followed then for a moment or two, for Orion looked lost in thought, swallowed by his memories, and Vivian was drowning in guilt, unable to live with herself. The decisions she'd made had driven her to this terrible place in her life, and no longer could she live with herself.

She couldn't stand it for another second.

Orion seemed to sense her decision and awoke from his wandering thoughts, casting his gaze yet again back over the young Featherstone he had sworn so unfalteringly to protect, even to the point of taking his own son's life.

He glanced over Vivian's body. It was in absolute tatters, and his examination drew her gaze too, and she looked herself over.

Her leg and arm and shoulder were still clearly ruined, though she had patched them back together enough to keep them in one piece. Her back was peppered along its full length with shards of stone and glass, which dug deeper and twisted further every time she moved. The scars that had knocked her spine still bled in horizontal streaks, and finally, as if that wasn't enough, her entire torso and the tops of her thighs had been sliced to shreds by Euan's claws, as he had desperately clung to her in his dying moments.

It was safe to say that young Vivian was in a sorry state. Her wounds no longer bled, for she had no more blood to lose, and the pain had almost entirely subsided, replaced by an empty numbness that she was growing evermore familiar with.

"The only thing keeping you alive is your power." Orion explained then.

Vivian remembered the sword through her ribs long ago, and how her body had simply continued doing as she instructed, even though it had been beyond saving, supposedly.

She still bore the scars as a reminder.

She nodded slowly in agreement. It was certainly not the first time she'd been beyond repair.

Glancing all around her briefly, Vivian scanned what she could see of the courtyard that bordered the Keep. The battle had clearly been hard fought, and she didn't like what she saw, for both sides had suffered terribly.

"I can't sense them any more…" She said then, almost as if she was thinking aloud.

"The plague?" Orion questioned.

"Yes." Vivian replied, nodding her head in response. "It's gone."

"That it is." The great dragon agreed. "I've been watching them ever since you killed the Grey." He began to explain. "Trying to kill them, or at least keep them in check."

"What happened?" Vivian asked.

"They hid themselves away from you. They knew you would surely come after them, and their power was no match for yours. But they've been biding their time. I tried, but their numbers grew too fast…" Orion explained, but this time Vivian cut him off.

"No." She interjected, shaking her head slowly. Orion had misunderstood her meaning. "What happened to Euan?"

The enormous dragon sighed deeply, exhaling his sorrow all too obviously on his warm breath.

"Euan had once been a part of the Redwoods." He began. "Just as all those others infected by the Greystone's plague had too."

Orion thought for a moment, looking around at his fellow creatures sat listening to the words he spoke.

"Euan was young, and brave, but foolish. He believed he could stop the plague from spreading. He didn't know the extent of its reach."

Orion sighed deeply, but continued nonetheless.

"Eventually, the more he fought those that were already infected by it, the more he succumbed to it. Finally, after a few years, he was so full of hate and twisted longing to kill you that he simply couldn't hide away any longer."

The great red dragon's words were heavy like lead, and they weighed down on Vivian and Orion terribly.

"But just as all the others once were…" Orion continued. "Euan had once been a part of the Redwoods, and so, when you summoned us, myself included, for you have so much power, we had no choice but to obey."

Vivian nodded slowly, understanding what Orion was saying, but unable to speak on it.

He inhaled deeply, sorrow filling his enormous lungs, and pressed on.

"And so now, because of your bravery, the Redwood Forest is finally safe once again." He concluded, bowing his head in acknowledgement to Vivian.

But this time Vivian found her tongue in an instant, and scorned at the great dragon's words.

"Bravery?" She scoffed. "I've shown no bravery today."

"Yes, Vivian, you have." Orion said then, his tone growing somehow even more serious. "I have seen none braver. Not even your great ancestor, William Featherstone, who changed the blood of the forests and of the animals, had the courage that you possess.

Vivian realised then that she was only the second Featherstone that Orion had ever revealed himself to, and that this was truly the most momentous of occasions.

"Thank you Orion." Vivian replied, her gratitude genuine. But her words were followed by a deep and weary sigh. "But I am so very sorry."

"Sorry?" The great dragon questioned, confused.

"Yes." Vivian admitted, nodding slowly. "I'm sorry that you'll never have the chance to meet another Featherstone. I'm sorry that there will never again be another descendant of my family. I'm sorry for all the harm I've caused." Tears welled in Vivian's eyes as she spoke now. "I never meant for anything but good to come of what I've done."

"Your power is weakened, Vivian, but it is vast!" Orion exclaimed. "I can feel it! You need only heal your injuries!"

But Vivian only shook her head.

"There isn't enough power in the whole world to heal the wounds I've suffered." She said then, her voice ominous. "They have been so great and so numerous that I've numbed myself from them, and from everything else."

Orion looked on, helpless in his dreadful realisation of what Vivian was saying.

"I don't want numbness any more, Orion." Vivian continued. "All that I feel besides that is the lust to kill, and that's more painful than any wound I could possibly suffer."

And then, as if to emphasise her point, Vivian looked down at her ravaged body, barely held together by thin shreds of skin.

"I've learned that from experience."

"But the Redwoods need you Vivian! Virtus needs you! The Redwoods Empire has always needed the Featherstones!"

Vivian just shook her head in disagreement.

"The Featherstones were only ever needed to balance out the Greystone's evil." Vivian explained to Orion, somehow gaining an understanding of such a complicated thing in the simplest of terms. "The people of Virtus saved themselves, and now they're thriving with purpose. The Greystones are gone: they don't need me anymore."

"But what about the Redwoods!?" Orion immediately asked, but again he was met only with disappointment.

"I summoned the creatures of the Redwoods…" Vivian continued. "But they fought the battle. You fought the battle!!" She exclaimed, her voice rising and falling dramatically.

As Vivian spoke she looked around again at all the creatures still surrounding her, looking on imploringly. They bore the scars of battle, but held their heads high with the pride of victory, their freedom now won.

Even Orion bled from his clash with Euan, for his powerful back legs shimmered with fresh blood oozing from puncture wounds where son had struggled and fought against father.

"And you've all succeeded!!" She suddenly revelled then. "You've won! And now you're free and safe to live in the knowledge of your victory!"

"But Vivian…" Orion attempted one last time, but he was silenced by Vivian's raised hand.

"The Greystones, and anything that remained of their evil, is gone now." She concluded ominously. "I'm no longer needed. The Featherstones are no longer needed. There is no more evil for us to fight. Our purpose is fulfilled."

At first there was only silence, bellowing without a sound at Vivian's prophetic words. It rippled through the ranks gathered all around like an invisible shockwave, stirring them all, but at the same time immobilising them.

Orion didn't reply at first, and his fellow kin all around looked on imploringly.

He had lived long enough however, known enough enemies, fought enough battles, and learned enough lessons, to know that Vivian's mind was set, and that, in fact, considering everything, probably more than he would ever know, she was right.

Vivian clambered slowly to her feet, willing her ruined body into motion once again. It obeyed her commands robotically, entirely ignorant of the fact that without her power urging it on, it simply would not be able to function.

Stumbling forwards, Vivian placed a weary and blood stained hand upon Orion's scaly shoulder, smiling affectionately up at the great dragon, thanking him with her eyes, not saying a word. She cast the same look out across the countless animals still frozen in time all around her, silently portraying her gratitude to each and every one of them.

Forcing her legs to move once more then, Vivian turned her back on Featherstone Keep for the last time, as she had always known she would do, never to return, and began calmly off into the trees, focusing all of her strength on simply staying on her feet.

Slowly, the woodlands around her thickened as she cut deeper and deeper into the great Redwood Forest. As the light from above faded as the canopy gradually thickened, Vivian slowly allowed her hold upon her vast, albeit weakening power, to steadily slip from her grasp.

The subtle strains on her will that were keeping what was left of her body functioning, subconsciously keeping her alive, dissipated bit by bit. She just let them drain away as she continued walking further and further into the endless sea of trees, the hundreds upon thousands of animals all around watching her remorsefully, with tears standing heavily in their eyes.

Then she was illuminated again by blinding moonlight, streaming in through an enormous break in the canopy. Her weary eyes fell then upon the body of Euan, blood stained and defeated, lifeless, spread out across the forest floor callously, where his father had been forced to abandon him to save her.

Vivian's pace slowed more and more and tears stood heavily in her eyes as she left Euan's body behind, brushing his massive shoulder lightly and sorrowfully with her hand as she passed.

Her pain did not lessen, and eyes only grew heavier as she felt her life begin to slip away.

Images of her mother and father, mixed with images of Red and Clover and Kael, and Emerson, the father she had never known, all flashed before her eyes then. For the briefest moment, lost amidst everything else, her senses were alive with the complete vision and smell and even touch of her loved ones.

She hoped she would see them again, in one form or another: in another life perhaps.

Knowing that both Virtus and the Redwoods were now safe, able to support themselves and grow and indeed thrive, no longer in need of her, no longer in need of protection, Vivian allowed her heavy responsibilities to thankfully drop away, filling her with almighty relief.

Now she too was free, and her thoughts wandered immediately to all those she had lost so terribly, and missed so dearly.

Vivian slipped gradually away into the darkness, both of the deepening and thickening Redwood trees all around her, and of the endless clutches of death consuming her.

As she finally allowed it to claim her, she was comforted by those happy thoughts of her family, and it was a great relief to finally be seized by the emptiness of death, freeing her from the long, lonely and painful torment of living.

Young Vivian Featherstone, fabled in folklore and legend from one end of the Redwood Empire to the other, had finally completed all that had been required of her.

Having endured and overcome her burdensome rise, Vivian's work was done, and she now gladly succumbed to her eventual, well deserved fall.

Thank you for reading The Redwoods Rise and Fall

I hope you enjoyed it

You may also enjoy:

Ross Turner

Voices in the Mirror

Evening encroached upon them and a deep, vast, endless darkness swept in upon the tiny, insignificant village of Riverbrook.

Cold winds cut through the trees and bit harshly at the exposed faces of anybody who dared still remain out under the enormous sky, scattered with an ocean of burned out stars that seethed and watched without a sound.

A million and more shining eyes that had gazed down upon the face of the Earth for a hundred millennia and even longer, turned their cruel eyes now to all that was unfolding before them, and for not the first time in history, something impossible and wonderful, a miracle, began to unfold.

Please visit my facebook and twitter pages for the latest updates

Ross Turner Books
@RossTurnerBooks

Printed in Great Britain
by Amazon

The Redwoods
Rise and Fall
Book Two

By Ross Turner

Lou/

Congratulations!

Thanks you for entering.

Enjoy!

Ross/

Ross Turner

©Ross Turner

For Kirsty,

Because you hold a very special place in my heart,
I'll always be here for you,

Love always,

Ross.

Ross Turner

And for Keely,

Because although we may be worlds apart,
You always put a smile on my face,

I miss you dearly,

Ross.